For Diane Pearson

NOT THE END OF THE WORLD

NOT THE END OF THE WORLD

KATE ATKINSON

Doubleday

LONDON · NEW YORK · TORONTO · SYDNEY · AUCKLAND

TRANSWORLD PUBLISHERS
61–63 Uxbridge Road, London W5 5SA
a division of The Random House Group Ltd

RANDOM HOUSE AUSTRALIA (PTY) LTD
20 Alfred Street, Milsons Point, Sydney,
New South Wales 2061, Australia

RANDOM HOUSE NEW ZEALAND LTD
18 Poland Road, Glenfield, Auckland 10, New Zealand

RANDOM HOUSE SOUTH AFRICA (PTY) LTD
Endulini, 5a Jubilee Road, Parktown 2193, South Africa

Published 2002 by Doubleday
a division of Transworld Publishers

'The Bodies Vest' first appeared in the *Daily Telegraph* in March 2001.
A (shorter) version of 'Tunnel of Fish' was a Radio 4/Edinburgh Book Festival commission and was first broadcast in August 2001.
'Charlene and Trudi Go Shopping' was a commission from the Ilkley Literary Festival and was first read there in October 2001.
The lines quoted on p. 126 are reprinted by permission of the publishers and the Trustees of the Loeb Classical Library from Hesiod: *Homeric Hymns. Epic Cycle, Homerica*, Loeb Classical Library Volume L 57, translated by Hugh Evelyn-White, Cambridge, Mass.: Harvard University Press, 1914. The Loeb Classical Library ® is a registered trademark of the President and Fellows of Harvard College.
The extract on p. 220 is from *Buffy the Vampire Slayer* © Twentieth Century Fox Television.
All rights reserved.

A catalogue record for this book is available from the British Library.
ISBNs 0385 604726 (cased)
0385 605196 (tpb)

Typeset in 11/15½pt Weiss by
Falcon Oast Graphic Art Ltd.

Printed in Great Britain
by Clays Ltd, St Ives plc

1 3 5 7 9 10 8 6 4 2

NOT THE END OF THE WORLD

KATE ATKINSON

Doubleday

LONDON · NEW YORK · TORONTO · SYDNEY · AUCKLAND

TRANSWORLD PUBLISHERS
61–63 Uxbridge Road, London W5 5SA
a division of The Random House Group Ltd

RANDOM HOUSE AUSTRALIA (PTY) LTD
20 Alfred Street, Milsons Point, Sydney,
New South Wales 2061, Australia

RANDOM HOUSE NEW ZEALAND LTD
18 Poland Road, Glenfield, Auckland 10, New Zealand

RANDOM HOUSE SOUTH AFRICA (PTY) LTD
Endulini, 5a Jubilee Road, Parktown 2193, South Africa

Published 2002 by Doubleday
a division of Transworld Publishers

'The Bodies Vest' first appeared in the *Daily Telegraph* in March 2001.
A (shorter) version of 'Tunnel of Fish' was a Radio 4/Edinburgh Book Festival commission and was first broadcast in August 2001.
'Charlene and Trudi Go Shopping' was a commission from the Ilkley Literary Festival and was first read there in October 2001.
The lines quoted on p. 126 are reprinted by permission of the publishers and the Trustees of the Loeb Classical Library from Hesiod: *Homeric Hymns. Epic Cycle, Homerica*, Loeb Classical Library Volume L 57, translated by Hugh Evelyn-White, Cambridge, Mass.: Harvard University Press, 1914. The Loeb Classical Library ® is a registered trademark of the President and Fellows of Harvard College.
The extract on p. 220 is from *Buffy the Vampire Slayer* © Twentieth Century Fox Television.
All rights reserved.

A catalogue record for this book is available from the British Library.
ISBNs 0385 604726 (cased)
0385 605196 (tpb)

Typeset in 11/15½pt Weiss by
Falcon Oast Graphic Art Ltd.

Printed in Great Britain
by Clays Ltd, St Ives plc

1 3 5 7 9 10 8 6 4 2

THANKS TO:

Laura Denby and Dr John Menzies for the telomeres
Helen Clyne for a lot of things
Russell Equi for cars and bikes and roads
Eve Atkinson-Worden for the weddings
Sally Wray for the support
Ali Smith for the understanding

ILLUSTRATION CREDITS

Frontispiece: *Private Collection/© Bridgeman Art Library*; I: *The Chimera of Arezzo*, woodcut; II: engraving from *Le Ballet Comique de la Reyne* by Balthasar Beaujoyeulx, Paris, 1582; III: *Atalanta* from *De Vernieuwde Gulden Winckel der kunstleibende Niederlanders* by Joost van den Vondel, 1622; IV: *Troilus*, sixteenth-century woodcut by the Master of the Standing Warrior; V: *Assembly of the Gods*, woodcut from Ovid's *Metamorphoses*, Leipzig, 1582; VI: Diana, engraving by Antonio Belema after Parmigianino; VII: woodcut from Albumasar's *Flores Astrologie*, 1488; VIII: woodcut from *Historium Animalium* by Conrad Gesner, 1551–58. © *Academy of Natural Sciences of Philadelphia/CORBIS*; IX: *In fidem uxoriam* from *Emblemata* by Andrea Alciatus, 1550; X: *Rape of Proserpina* by Cherubino Alberti; XI: *Hymen* from *Le Imagini, con la spositione de i dei de gli antichi* by Vincenzo Cartari, 1580; XII: *Poliphilus and Polia among the nymphs at the Fountain of Venus* from *Poliphili Hypnerotomachia* by Francesco Colonna, 1499.

I

CHARLENE AND TRUDI GO SHOPPING

In nova fert animus mutatas dicere formas
corpora; di, coeptis (nam vos mutastis et illas)
adspirate meis primaque ab origine mundi
ad mea perpetuum deducite tempora carmen

OVID, *METAMORPHOSES* BOOK I, 1–4

For Sally

'I WANT,' CHARLENE SAID TO TRUDI, 'TO BUY MY mother a birthday present.'

'OK,' Trudi said.

'Something I can put in the post. Something that won't break.'

Trudi thought about some of the things you could put in the post that might break:

A crystal decanter.

A fingernail.

An egg.

A heart.

A Crown Derby teapot.

A promise.

A mirrored-glass globe in which nothing but the sky is reflected.

'How about a scarf?' she suggested. 'In velvet dévoré. I

love that word. Dévoré.'

Charlene and Trudi were in a food hall as vast as a small city. It smelt of chocolate and ripe cheese and raw meaty bacon but most of the food was too expensive to buy and some of it didn't look real. They wandered along an avenue of honey.

'I could buy a jar of honey,' Trudi said.

'You could,' Charlene agreed.

There was plenty of honey to choose from. There was lavender honey and rosemary honey, acacia and orange blossom and mysterious manuka. Butter-yellow honey from Tuscan sunflowers and thick, anaemic honey from English clover. There were huge jars like ancient amphorae and neat spinster-sized pots. There were jars of cut-comb honey that looked like seeded amber. There was organic honey from lush South American rainforests and there was honey squeezed from parsimonious Scottish heather on windswept moorlands. Bees the world over had been bamboozled out of their bounty so that Trudi could have a choice, but she had already lost interest.

'You could buy her soap,' Trudi said. 'Soap wouldn't break. Expensive soap. Made from oatmeal and buttermilk or goat's milk and vanilla pods from . . . wherever vanilla pods come from.'

'Mauritius. Mainly,' Charlene said.

'If you say so. Soap for which ten thousand violet petals have been crushed and distilled to provide one drop of oil.

Or soap scented with the zest of a hundred bittersweet oranges.'

'I'm hungry. I could buy an orange,' Charlene said.

'You could. Seville or Moroccan?'

'Moorish,' Charlene said dreamily. 'I would like to visit a Moorish palace. The Alhambra. That's an exotic word. That's the most exotic word I can think of, offhand. Alhambra.'

'Xanadu,' Trudi said. 'That's exotic. A pleasure dome. Imagine having your own pleasure dome. You could call it Pleasureland. Isn't there a Pleasureland in Scarborough?'

'Arbroath,' Charlene said gloomily.

'With shady walks through cool gardens,' Trudi said, 'where the air is perfumed with attar of roses.'

'And fountains and courtyards,' Charlene said. 'Fountains that run with nectar. And courtyards full of peacocks and nightingales and larks. And swans. And gold and silver fish swimming in the fountains. And huge blue and white marbled carp.'

They were walking down a street of teas. They were lost.

'Who would think there were so many different teas in the world?' Trudi mused. 'Chrysanthemum tea, White Peony, Jade Peak, Oriental Beauty Oolong, Green Gunpowder, Golden Needle, Hubei Silver Tip, Drum Mountain White Cloud, Dragon's Breath tea – do you think it tastes of dragon's breath? What do you think dragon's breath tastes like?'

'Foul, I expect,' Charlene said. 'And all day long,' she continued, 'in the pleasure dome—'

'Pleasureland,' Trudi corrected.

'Pleasureland. We would eat melon and figs and scented white peaches and Turkish Delight and candied rose petals.'

'And drink raspberry sherbet and tequila and Canadian ice wine,' Trudi enthused.

'I should go,' Charlene said. She had failed to recover her spirits since the mention of Arbroath. 'I've got an article to write.' Charlene was a journalist with a bridal magazine. 'Ten Things To Consider Before You Say "I Do".'

'Saying "I Don't"?' Trudi suggested.

'Abracadabra,' Charlene murmured to herself as she crossed against the traffic in the rain, 'that's an exotic word.' Somewhere in the distance a bomb exploded softly.

It had been raining for weeks. There were no taxis outside the radio station. Charlene was worried that she was developing a crush on the man who searched her handbag in the reception at the radio station.

'I know he's quite short,' she said to Trudi, 'but he's sort of manly.'

'I once went out with a short man,' Trudi said. 'I never realized just how short he was until after I'd left him.' There were no taxis at the rank. There were no taxis dropping anyone off at the radio station.

Trudi frowned. 'When did you last see a taxi?'

Charlene and Trudi ran from the radio station, ran from the rain, past the sandbags lining the streets, into the warm, dispassionate space of the nearest hotel and sat in the smoky lounge and ordered tea.

'I think he's ex-military or something.'

'Who?'

'The man who searches the bags at the radio station.'

A waitress brought them weak green tea. They sipped their tea daintily – an adverb dictated by the awkward handles of the cups.

'I've always wanted to go out with a man in a uniform,' Trudi said.

'A fireman,' Charlene suggested.

'Mm,' Trudi said thoughtfully.

'Or a policeman,' Charlene said.

'But not a constable.'

'No, not a constable,' Charlene agreed. 'An inspector.'

'An army captain,' Trudi said, 'or maybe a naval helicopter pilot.'

The weak green tea was bitter.

'This could be Dragon's Breath tea, for all we know,' Trudi said. 'Do you think it is? Dragon's breath?'

There was no air in the hotel. Two large, middle-aged women were eating scones with quiet determination. A well-known journalist was seducing a girl who was too young. Two very old men were speaking in low pleasant tones to each other about music and ancient wars.

'Thermopylae,' the men murmured. 'Aegospotami, Cumae. The "Dissonant Quartet".'

'I really want a cat,' Trudi said.

'You can't keep a cat in town,' Charlene said.

'You can't keep a cat down?'

'You can't keep a cat in *town*.'

'You can.'

'You need something small like a rodent,' Charlene said.

'A capybara's a rodent, it's not small.'

'A hamster,' Charlene said, 'a gerbil, a small white mouse.'

'I don't want a rodent. Of any size. I want a cat. Kitty, kitty, kitty, kitty, kitty. If you say something five times you always get it.'

'You made that up,' Charlene said.

'True,' Trudi admitted.

'I'd like something more unusual,' Charlene said. 'A kangaroo. A reindeer or an otter. A talking bird or a singing fish.'

'A singing fish?'

'A singing fish. A fish that sings and has a magic ring in its stomach. A huge carp that is caught in a fishpond – usually at a royal court somewhere – and cooked and served at the table and when you bite into the fish you find a magic ring. And the magic ring will lead you to the man who will love you. Or the small white mouse which is the disguise of the man who will love you.'

'That would be a rodent then.'

'Failing that,' Charlene continued, ignoring Trudi, 'I would like a cat as big as a man.'

'A cat as big as a man?' Trudi frowned, trying to picture a man-sized cat.

'Yes. Imagine if men had fur.'

'I think I'd rather not.'

The waitress asked them if they wanted more of the weak green tea.

'For myself,' the waitress said, uninvited, 'I prefer dogs.' Charlene and Trudi swooned with delight at the idea of dogs.

'Oh God,' Trudi said, overcome by all the breeds of dog in the world, 'a German Shepherd, a Golden Retriever, a Great Dane, a Borzoi – what a great word – a St Bernard, a Scottie, a Westie, a Yorkie. An Austrian Pinscher, a Belgian Griffon, a Kromfohrlanders. The Glen of Imaal Terrier, the Manchester, Norwich, English Toy, Staffordshire, Bedlington – all terriers also. The Kai, the Podengo Portugueso Medio, the Porcelaine and the Spanish Greyhound. The Bloodhound, the Lurcher, the Dunker, the Catahoula Leopard Dog, the Hungarian Vizsla, the Lancashire Heeler and the Giant German Spitz!'

'Or a mongrel called Buster or Spike,' Charlene said.

The waitress cleared away their tea things. 'Money,

money, money, money, money,' she whispered to herself as she bumped open the door to the kitchen with her hip. The electricity failed and everyone was suddenly very quiet. No one had realized how dark the rain had made the afternoon.

In the reception at the television station there was a tank of fish so big that it covered a whole wall. Trudi noted that they were mostly African freshwater fish. She wondered if they had flown here in a plane and if that had felt strange for them. No one else was taking any notice of the wall of fish. The receptionist had strawberry-blond hair, coiffed extravagantly. She appeared to have a Heckler and Koch MP5A3 9mm sub-machine gun under her desk. Trudi felt a wave of jealousy.

Trudi was a publicist for a small imprint in a large publishing house. She had a twin sister called Heidi and neither Trudi nor Heidi liked their names. They were the names (in the opinion of Heidi and Trudi) of goat-herding girls and American hookers, of girls who wore their hair in plaits and drank milk or had sex dressed as French maids and nurses. Of girls who never grew up. Trudi and Heidi had no idea why they were so called. Their parents had died in a bizarre accident not long after they were born and the kind strangers who stood in for them, Mr and Mrs Marshall, had no insight into their dead parents' thoughts.

Charlene and Trudi ordered gin slings and picked at a small dish of black olives that tasted more bitter than weak green tea.

There were boisterous men in suits perched at the bar. They were wondering how drunk they could get in the pre-curfew swill.

'I need a new haircut,' Charlene said.

'I need new hair,' Trudi said.

'And thinner ankles,' Charlene said.

'And bigger breasts,' Trudi said. 'Or maybe I want smaller breasts.'

'Your breasts are perfect.'

'Thank you.'

They could smell the perfume of the women sitting at the adjacent table, peppery and spicy with a top note of deodorant. The women were dressed in very fashionable, very ugly clothes. People stared at them because their clothes were so fashionable and so ugly. They smoked incessantly and drank Martinis. There was an oily film on top of their drinks. They looked like high-class whores but they were rock stars' ex-wives.

A waiter dropped a tray of glasses. The boisterous men in suits dangled their cigarettes from their mouths while they applauded.

'And,' Trudi said, 'I would like to ride on a horse-drawn

sleigh through forests in the snow with dogs – Borzois – running alongside and I want to be wearing silks and velvets and a cloak lined with the fur of Arctic foxes and bears and wolfkins—'

'You mean wolf skins?'

'No, wolfkins – they're very rare – but only ones that have died of natural causes, not ones that have been killed for their fur.'

'Of course not.'

'And diamonds, old rose-cut diamonds like dark, melting ice, at my throat and ears, and on my fingers, rubies and opals like larks' eggs, and on my feet red leather seven-league boots—'

'Flat or with a heel?'

'A modest heel. And I want to drink a liqueur made from ripe purple plums from a silver hip flask and—' One of the boisterous men in suits fell off his bar stool. The barman pronounced his time of death as 9.42 p.m.

'Time to go home, ladies and gentlemen,' he said, 'time to go home.'

Later, Charlene wished she had asked Trudi what a wolfkin was.

Charlene worried that she would never have a baby. A baby would love her. A baby would exactly fit the round hollow space inside her. That might be a problem when it grew, of course. 'Baby, baby, baby, baby, baby,' she said to the mirror before she went to bed.

First, of course, she had to get someone to father the baby and after the humiliating ordeal with the dead solicitor last year she couldn't imagine ever having sex again. This worried her less than she would have imagined. Before. And Charlene would call the baby Smiler. A boy. As fat as a porker, as big as a bomb.

In the hours between curfew and dawn Charlene listened to the sirens wailing through the night and planned an article on 'Great Tips For Spring Weddings'. She fell asleep with her hand on the Sig Sauer semi-automatic she kept under her pillow and didn't wake until Eosphorus, the morning star, rose and heralded the coming of his mother, Eos, the dawn.

Trudi was looking for black trousers. Something simple by Joseph or perhaps Nicole Farhi. Charlene took trousers from the racks in the department store and displayed them with a sales assistant's flourish for Trudi to view. All the genuine sales assistants seemed to have disappeared. Trudi didn't like any of the trousers Charlene showed her.

'Perhaps you could take the trousers from an Armani suit

and leave the jacket?' Charlene suggested. 'Or MaxMara – they have a lot of black suits this season. Well cut. I think I'm quite good at this, don't you? Perhaps I could do this for a living.'

All the black clothes were sprinkled with plaster dust like dandruff.

'From the earthquake, probably,' Charlene said. 'They really should be on sale, not full price.'

Trudi tried on a Moschino dress and a Prada jacket and a Kenzo cardigan and a Gucci skirt but all the clothes were made for tiny, whippet-thin Japanese girls.

'I'll never go to the ball,' Trudi said sadly.

'The balls were all cancelled long ago, as you well know,' Charlene said briskly. 'Try this Betty Jackson wrap.'

In the end, Trudi decided to buy a rhinestone belt but there were no sales assistants to buy it from and unlike nearly everyone else in the city she wasn't a thief.

'We should make clothes,' Charlene said as they passed through the haberdashery floor of the department store.

'What a wonderful word,' Trudi said.

'What a wonderful world?' Charlene said doubtfully.

'No. *Word*. Haberdashery.'

'We could buy a sewing machine and share it,' Charlene said. 'We could buy cloth and spools of thread and paper patterns and spend pleasant winter evenings dressmaking together. Perhaps by the soft light from beautiful glass oil-lamps. We could sit in a pool of golden light from the beautiful glass oil-lamps and our silver needles would glimmer and flash as we bowed our heads to the simple yet honest work.'

But Trudi was looking at the bolts of cloth, shelf after shelf of every different kind of fabric. 'Goodness,' she said, 'this is very impressive. Broadcloth and butter muslin, brocade, brocatelle, buckram, bunting and Botany wool. Bombazine and bouclé, burlap and Bedford cord, barège, bobbinet, balbriggan and barathea! And that's just the Bs. Then, there's cambric and calico and cavalry twill—'

The tannoy started up with a sudden howl of feedback and a disembodied voice announced that it was looking for Mr Scarlet. 'Would Mr Scarlet please come to haberdashery, Mr Scarlet to haberdashery, please.'

Charlene started to panic. 'You know what that means, don't you?' she said to Trudi.

'No. What does it mean?'

'It's the code for a fire. It means there's a fire in haberdashery.'

'I don't see any fire,' Trudi said. 'Wouldn't we see smoke? No fire without smoke, isn't that what they say?'

'No, they don't say that.'

Sales assistants suddenly appeared from wherever they had been lurking, driven out like rats by the invisible fire. Even if she couldn't see it, Trudi could imagine the fire. She could see the apocalyptic television images of ash and soot, the blobs of grease and molten steel raining down on their heads, she could smell the excessively combustible materials in haberdashery catching and flaming, she could feel the black smoke choking them. Perhaps they could wrap themselves in the bolts of cloth, like the poor Bangkok sweatshop girls Trudi had read about – hoping that their fall would be cushioned as they threw themselves from the building, as they threw themselves away. Trudi wondered if they would unravel as they fell, like bobbins unwinding, like Egyptian mummies unravelling through the air.

'Or we could lead an even simpler life,' Charlene said hurriedly, 'a life where there are no machines and where we would live on a green hillside and sleep under the stars and gather kindling in the woods. And we would keep animals—'

'What kind of animals?' Trudi asked, as everything from taffeta to winceyette suddenly went up in flames.

'Goats,' Charlene said decisively. 'We'll keep goats. We'll tend goats on the green hillside and milk them and make goats' cheese and at night we'll light bonfires and guard the goats against the wolves. And we'll buy a spinning wheel and spin the goats' wool and knit jumpers and every week we'll take our goats' jumpers and our goats' cheeses to market and people will buy them and that's how we'll live.'

There was a flashover in Ladies' Fashions.

'I knew I should have taken that rhinestone belt,' Trudi said regretfully.

The radio station was off air. The television station had been destroyed a long time ago. The city ran out of diesel and gin. People burnt musty old paperbacks on bonfires and drank rum. There was a festive atmosphere generated by communal terror.

There was no food for the animals in the zoo. The animal freedom militia unlocked their cages so that now there were bears rooting in dustbins and penguins swimming in the river and at night the tigers roaming the streets roared so loudly that no one could sleep. Trudi lay awake listening to the tigers roaring and the bears growling and the wolves howling and the dragons breathing fire over the blacked-out, rain-sodden streets of the city. A family of small green lizards took up residence in her apartment.

There was a rumour that the rare wolfkin had been sighted in the botanical gardens in the west of the city. All the trees in the botanical gardens were now officially dead. And all the panes of glass in the hothouses were broken so that the rain came in and drenched the plants in the desert house causing them to bloom extravagantly and then die, even more extravagantly. An unseasonal microclimate in the palm house resulted in a typhoon snapping the great palms that had been alive longer than anyone on the planet. A polar bear made its home on the island in the middle of the lake in the botanical gardens and a flock of parrots flitted in and out of the pagoda.

The museums were no longer policed and people wandered in and took the artefacts and used them to improve their interior décor.

Charlene came to dinner and brought Trudi the golden death mask of a long dead king and also a large Sèvres bowl that had taken her fancy. 'Thief,' Trudi said, but hoarsely, as they were both still suffering from the after-effects of smoke inhalation during the department-store fire.

All Trudi had in the house to eat was roasted buckwheat and celery. They served the buckwheat and the celery in the Sèvres bowl.

'Presentation is everything,' Charlene said. Afterwards, they drank the only thing they could find, which was a bottle of emerald-green Midori, and listened to a Mozart string quartet on a foreign radio station. Charlene stayed the night, lying on the sofa, watching the lizards run across the ceiling. In the skylight above her head she could see a few drops of the Milky Way, which she knew was the milk from Hera's breasts splashed across the heavens.

Charlene was pinned down by sniper fire in the north of the city on her way back from visiting a wedding fair. She still had a selection of wedding samples in her coat pocket – metallic confetti in the form of the names 'Mark' and 'Rachel', a placecard in the shape of a top hat, a little silver favour basket of red jelly hearts and a bonbonnière containing sugared almonds in pastel colours. She took shelter in the doorway of a bank and phoned Trudi on her Samsung A400.

'A bonbonnière?' Trudi said doubtfully.

'Or bomboniere if you prefer the Italian. In pink shadow crystal net with red roses.'

'Why?'

'A bonbonnière makes a wonderful way of saying "Thank you" for sharing the joy of your day. Each bonbonnière contains five top quality sugared almonds, five being a prime number which cannot be divided, just like the bride and groom—'

'OK.'

'They signify happiness, health, wealth, fertility and long life—'

'Enough.'

'When I get married,' Charlene said, 'I want white satin wedding shoes, silver horseshoes with white heather, lucky black cats and a bouquet of lilacs dripping with rain. Oh, and a sprung wooden floor to dance on and a father to give me away and a mother to cry and a sister to be bridesmaid – but I have none of these, neither father nor mother nor sister.'

'Nor bridegroom,' Trudi reminded her.

'Thank you.'

'I'll give you away,' Trudi offered, 'and I'll cry and I'll be your bridesmaid.'

'Thank you.'

The ATM in the wall exploded and banknotes fluttered like distressed birds into the dirty sky. Charlene tried to remember the tenets of Pythagorean philosophy to keep her mind off the rain and the sniper and the flying money.

'When you rise from the bedclothes, roll them together and smooth out the impress of the body.

'The visible world is false and illusive.

'Abstain from beans.'

'Beans?'

'In case they contain the soul of an ancestor.'

'Of course.'

'Men and women are equal and property held in common.

'All things are numbers.

'Everything is infinitely divisible and even the smallest portion of matter contains some of each element.'

'And the transmigration of the soul,' Trudi whispered, 'don't forget that. When you get home, call me.' A cashier ran out of the bank waving a Colt Defender and was freeze-framed. Charlene wondered about Mark and Rachel. Did they exist or had the people who made the wedding favours (for which occupation there seemed to be no word) invented them, as an ideal couple?

Lying awake in the dark, Charlene wished she had a lamp to wish on.

'See the moon? See Selene's silver beams?' she whispered

to Trudi although she knew Trudi couldn't hear her because the telephone exchange was burning and melting and the mobile-phone masts were toppled and anyway Trudi was asleep on the other side of town behind the barricades of wires and running shoes and dead dogs, mostly mongrels.

'I would like to be on the moon,' Charlene murmured, 'but with oxygen, or better still an atmosphere. And food. Or perhaps I would like a planet all of my own. But you could live there too, Trudi. We could call it Pleasureland. And we would be gods. We would be the gods of Pleasureland. And live there for ever.

'Or perhaps there's another world – except it's just like this one – where we buy French wine and sourdough bread and Moroccan oranges and spools of thread and packets of Drum Mountain White Cloud tea and sleep in our beds at night to the peaceful sounds of traffic and barking dogs and midnight arguments between husbands and wives called Mark and Rachel. That would be a good world to live in.'

Charlene and Trudi were drinking tall lattes and eating sunrise muffins in a coffee shop.

'So what did you get your mother for her birthday?' Trudi asked.

'Guess.'

'A Glock 17 semi-automatic?'

'No.'

'A mirrored-glass globe in which nothing but the sky is reflected?'

'No.'

'A carp? A harp? A sharp silver knife? A sliver of melon or a slice of yellow moon? A Spanish greyhound? A cat as big as a man, a man as big as a cat? As small as a baby? A manikin?'

'Gloves,' Charlene said.

'Gloves?'

'Yes,' Charlene said. 'Wolfkin gloves.'

II

TUNNEL OF FISH

Joy and Woe are woven fine,
A Clothing for the Soul divine
Under every grief and pine
Runs a joy with silken twine.

WILLIAM BLAKE, *AUGURIES OF INNOCENCE*

IF EDDIE COULD HAVE CHOSEN, HE WOULD HAVE BEEN a fish. A large fish without enemies, free to spend all day swimming lazily amongst the reeds and rushes in clear, blood-cold water. His mother, June, said not to worry, he was halfway there already, with his mouth hanging open all the time like a particularly dull-witted amphibian, not to mention the thick lenses of his spectacles that made his eyes bulge like a haddock's.

Afterwards, of course, June had regretted saying that, but sometimes Eddie was so infuriatingly gormless that she couldn't help herself. June had hoped that the removal of his adenoids when he was eight would make Eddie look more intelligent. It hadn't. She had had the same expectations at nine for his spectacles. Most people she knew looked brainier with glasses, yet somehow Eddie contrived to look even more dopey. June thought that the grommets in his ears at ten would raise him from the undersea world of the deaf, and theoretically they had done, according to his ENT consultant, yet Eddie still behaved as if he couldn't hear a word June said. Which was just as well, June thought, seeing as half the time the things she said to him were not very nice.

For reasons best known to himself, Eddie had recently become an obsessive cataloguer of fish. He had already worked his way through shells, coins, stamps and flags. June wondered, not for the first time, if Eddie was mildly autistic. She hoped his eccentricities were genetic and nothing to do with her haphazard mothering.

It was a year now since Eddie had started secondary school and every day June expected a policeman at the door, telling her that her son had been beaten to a pulp in a corner of the playground or thrown himself in boyish despair from the top of the science block. (June was a pessimist by nature.) Eddie, June knew, was exactly the sort of boy whom even kind children were exasperated into bullying and normally decent teachers were driven to persecute. In some ways it was a relief when, at the school's first parents' evening, June discovered that none of Eddie's teachers had any idea who he was.

June was carrying Hawk's child. She liked that phrase, 'carrying a child'. 'Pregnant' made her think of animals – cows and sows and dogs, and the hamster ('Hammy') which was the only pet her parents would let her have when she was a child because both of them were ridden with allergies. She had felt sorry for Hammy's solitary existence, mirroring her own, and had let him play with her friend's hamster, Jock, and 'play' turned out to be a euphemism and 'him' turned out to be a 'her' and the outcome was that June ended up with a litter of tiny naked rodents that looked like miniature piglets and which gave her the creeps. 'Oh, June,' her mother sighed when she saw them. That was what she always said – 'Oh, June' – so much disappointment packed into two such small words.

June didn't inherit her parents' allergies although that didn't stop them from expecting her to drop dead at any moment, if not of an out-of-the-blue asthma attack then from choking on a sweet or being run over by a car (or a bike or a train, not to mention being decapitated by a low-flying plane, as if such things were common in Edinburgh). Her father was a risk assessor for Standard Life and said that he came across too many accidents, bizarre or otherwise, to ignore the danger that lurked around every corner. The worst thing was that having spent her childhood and adolescence shrugging off their pathetic fears she was completely prey to them herself now.

June blamed her parents. June blamed her parents for everything, although it seemed a bit of a shame to blame her father, who had died in his bed, not from an accident but 'worn out' according to June's mother. 'By what?' June asked. 'By his life,' her mother said. His standard life. That was the one thing that June had been terrified of having – a standard life, an ordinary life, a life like her parents' – living in a pink sandstone semi-detached villa in the suburbs with a neat garden and an en-suite master bedroom with fitted wardrobes. Now she would rather like it. In their flat they didn't even have a bath, just a shower and a toilet. And a wardrobe, fitted or otherwise, would have been a great improvement on the overloaded garment rail on which they all kept their clothes.

And also June could see that once you were thirty – which she was three weeks ago – it was probably time to stop holding your parents responsible for all the things that had gone wrong in your life, especially as if she had taken their advice she would now have a degree and a job and a decent house and probably even a husband instead of living in a crappy tenement with Eddie and Hawk, and Hawk only living with them anyway because he didn't have anywhere else to live.

There was the dog as well, which didn't help. Tammy was an overenthusiastic terrier-cross that she'd got from the dogs' home at Seafield so that Eddie wouldn't have to spend his childhood without a pet the way she had, but then of course it turned out that the allergies had only skipped a generation and Eddie snuffled and sneezed and wheezed every time the dog got near him, which was all the time because the flat was so small. And the dog was pregnant. Carrying puppies.

June was just eighteen when she had Eddie (what a big, sorrowful 'Oh, June' that was) whereas her mother was forty-two when she had June. June fully expected to be dead by the time she was forty-two. Her parents were old, really old. That was why they'd given her such an old-fashioned name. June, because she was born in June. If she'd been born in November would they have called her November? June was a name for women in sitcoms and soap operas, the name of women who knit with synthetic wool and follow recipes that use cornflakes, not the name of a thirty-year-old with a ring in her nose ('Oh, June').

At least she knew she was pregnant this time – for the first five months of Eddie's unfledged existence she had just thought she was getting disgustingly fat. Of course, June had never really wanted Eddie and in her heart she was sure that had she wanted him he would have turned out a different child – a loud, rude, shouting boy who ran around football pitches and had no fear and no defects. June knew that Hawk's baby was her second chance, the only way she could redeem herself for the mess she had made the first time round.

Eddie wanted to scramble back down the evolutionary ladder. He wanted gills instead of a clogged-up nose. And scales of silver and pearl instead of his own pale-and-prone-to-dermatitis skin. Eddie wondered if there was such a word as 'unevolving'. He had a list of Latin prefixes in the ancient

Latin grammar that Hawk had found in a skip and he had been trying to teach himself the language ever since. Eddie didn't go to the kind of school where Latin had ever featured on the curriculum. There was a mystical power to Latin names. When he incanted the gorgeously impenetrable names of fish – *Pomacanthus imperator* (the Emperor Angelfish), *Zandus cornutus* (the Moorish Idol!) – Eddie felt like a sorcerer.

In-volve, re-volve, de-volve. Eddie pored over the grammar and stroked an imaginary beard. '"Retro-volve", perhaps, professor,' he said out loud to himself in a silly voice. Most of Eddie's conversations were with himself. His mother thought he was being bullied at school but Eddie knew he wasn't important enough in the school hierarchy to be bullied. He was part of the ranks of the invisible, but it was OK, there were quite a lot of invisible boys, they formed an unofficial, invisible club. They made feeble jokes to themselves about themselves – the Ancient Geeks, Geek Gods – and they all secretly believed that the geeks would inherit the earth.

A few months ago, Hawk had found an old fish tank and a goldfish to put in it but the fish had never thrived and had acquired all kinds of strange lumps and fungal growths until it was a relief when it went bleached and belly-up and put Eddie out of his misery. That was pretty much when Eddie had lost faith in Hawk. He knew how to get things but he didn't how to keep them.

Hawk's real name was 'Alan' which didn't have the same heroic ring to it. Hawk was English, from Cheshire, a place that was a mystery to both June and Eddie, who could think only of cheese and cats. His raptorial soubriquet was the result of a night in a sweat lodge in the Highlands when his true self – the hawk-headed sun god Ra – was revealed to him. 'Kind of like a totem,' he explained to Eddie. Eddie didn't tell Hawk that he also knew his own true identity – revealed to him by a huge, solid carp, patterned like blue and white marble, that lived in a pond in the hothouses in the Botanics. Eddie knew it was his totem because it had spoken to him.

Eddie often thought about the baby inside June. He had been charting its embryonic progress with an old medical encyclopaedia from the same skip haul as his Latin grammar. From tiny tadpole to gilled fish to froggy foetus, he had wondered about his unborn sibling. Brother or sister, he hadn't really minded, he just thought that it would be nice to have someone else in his family. Now it seemed it was going to be a girl, which Eddie thought would probably be better for his mother. He kept the ultrasound photograph of his soon-to-be sister by the side of his bed.

June rubbed baby oil onto her stomach. The skin on her belly was like a drum. The drum was being beaten from the inside in an irregular tom-tom and she wondered if the baby was kicking or punching. The baby was a girl. The technician doing the ultrasound had asked her did she want to know the sex or did she want to be surprised. June hated surprises. She had been surprised enough when she found out she was pregnant with Eddie. She wasn't surprised this time because she had stopped taking the pill and she pretty much only had to look at a man and, hey presto, she was pregnant. Carrying.

Sometimes June wondered if she attracted fertility. In the olden days she would probably have been burned as a sacrifice or something to help the crops.

Eddie wasn't her first. There was the sexless embryo that had had to be disposed of when she was fifteen ('Oh, June'). Her mother had tried to persuade her to keep it but June was having none of it. Now she thought about it a lot. A 'foetus', she'd taught herself to say over the years, but now it had become a baby again in her mind. Not that she was against abortions in any way. Terminated. It always made her think of Arnold Schwarzenegger. She was the terminator. It would have been fourteen and it wouldn't be an it, it would be a boy or a girl, an older brother or sister for Eddie, someone to guide him and be a friend (and, God knows, he could do with one). Maybe that was why she was having this baby. To make up. To atone.

Hawk was very surprised by her pregnancy, of course, because he didn't know about her coming off the pill and she told him it must have stopped working because she was sick that one time. She hoped the baby would make Hawk stay. Clip his wings. Although she knew it wouldn't.

She was glad it was a girl because she hadn't had much success with a boy. She could buy pretty clothes for a girl and plait her hair with ribbons. And she could call her a nice, old-fashioned, middle-class name like Sarah or Emma or Hannah. A girl would like dolls and ice-skating and ballet lessons. A girl would read novels and stories, not old encyclopaedias from skips. A girl would want to learn French knitting and the recorder and how to make a cake (that bit might be difficult). In fact, a girl would want the childhood that June had once had, the one she had despised so much when she became a teenager. Would her daughter grow up and treat her the way June treated her own mother? That would be ironic, wouldn't it, like punishment fitting the crime. The baby gave her a double punch, right upper cut, left hook. Perhaps it wouldn't be the kind of girl that June imagined. That would serve her right too.

She conceived Eddie on holiday. Things had never been the same for June after she terminated that foetus. She'd been top of her class at Watson's before but afterwards she lost interest in academic achievement. She'd limped on to the end of school and gone on holiday to Greece with a group of friends from her class. To Crete, although she'd never been sure where that was on the map. Eddie knew where it was on the map because he'd asked her, straight out, 'Where was I conceived?' She'd caught him reading one of her baby books (she wished she could get Hawk to read one). It seemed unnatural for a boy of his age to be interested in things like that. June wondered if it was a sign that he was gay. She wouldn't mind if he was, it was neither here nor there, she was all for gays – the more the better in fact – as long as it didn't make his life more difficult than it already was.

Eddie had been reading June's baby books. He thought it was odd that women had to read books to know how to be a mother, although he could see that his own mother needed a bit of a hand. He was looking forward to helping with the baby. If he helped with her she would love him even more. And he'd be a big brother, a hero to her. He liked the idea of being a hero.

He supposed she had been conceived in his mother's big, never-made bed. He knew the mechanics of it and he could hear them at it all the time. It had obviously never struck his mother that if she could say 'Eddie, come in here' from her bedroom without raising her voice and he could hear her in his own bedroom (although he usually pretended he couldn't), then it was more than likely that he was also going to hear her when she was yelling her head off in there going, 'Ohgod, ohgod, ohgod.' It wasn't clever and it wasn't funny, as Mrs McFarlane, his English teacher, would have said.

Eddie, on the other hand, had been conceived on the

island of Crete, which was Greek and in the Mediterranean and to which he hoped to sail one day on a fast wooden boat with a white sail like a wing. He had a book called an *Ancient Greek Primer* which he'd found in a jumble sale, but if he'd thought Latin was difficult then Greek took the biscuit, as his grandmother would have said. But it was beautiful to look at. They had done 'Ode to a Grecian Urn' in English, which had proved a bit too advanced for them, as Mrs McFarlane herself had admitted, but not before breaking down in tears, although that was probably because of her divorce rather than the Grecian Urn, but he had remembered the thing about beauty and truth because it seemed profound, which was his word of the week.

Tammy lay on her back with her legs in the air while he tickled her huge stomach. She looked as if she was going to burst any minute. He'd had to get a book out of the library on dogs because it didn't look as if either Hawk or his mother was going to make an effort to find out about whatever the word for dogs was. Puppybirth. Ha ha ha.

Another parents' evening. Surely one a year was enough. June found schools oppressive, all those female teachers looking at her, wondering how old she was when she had Eddie, judging her. It was such a schemie school. She wished she could afford to live somewhere better, send Eddie to a good school. His life would be different (his future would be different) if he went somewhere like

Watson's, the teachers would take more interest in him, care about him more. At least a few more of the teachers knew who Eddie was now. 'Eddie's developing quite a personality,' his science teacher said. What did that mean? 'Eddie,' his maths teacher ruminated, 'he's quite the comedian, isn't he?' (It was *never* good when they said that.) 'Eddie never seems to be quite *with* us,' the French teacher said, 'but he's pleasant enough.'

'Are you all right?' his English teacher asked her. She made a sympathetic face at June, cocking her head on one side and smiling at her. 'I can get you a cup of tea, if you want?' she offered. 'I remember how tiring it is when you're carrying such a weight around.' It took June a second to realize she meant the baby. June had left her contacts out and she squinted to see the English teacher's name on the handwritten sign in front of her. 'No thanks, Mrs . . . McFarlane.' June felt about six years old. 'Oh, call me Pam,' the English teacher said cheerfully, 'everyone else does,' and June felt glad that 'Pam' was one of Eddie's teachers because she seemed the caring sort, but then she saw that little frown pinching her round maternal features as she said, 'Eddie . . .' and June could see that she couldn't remember which one he was.

Despite her plump, mumsy look, she had a neurotic air about her – exactly the kind of woman June had always dreaded turning into. 'One minute they're a bump,' Mrs McFarlane laughed, 'and the next minute they're huge teenagers. And then they're gone.' She leant across the table in a conspiratorial way. June shrank back. 'Make the most of every day,' 'Pam' said. 'Every day is precious.'

'Yeah, right,' June said.

June couldn't imagine Eddie leaving home. He was days away from his twelfth birthday. Every time Eddie had a birthday June tried – and usually failed – to disguise the fact that he had hardly any relatives and no friends at all. In order to increase his pathetic tally of cards, even June's mother sent him two birthday cards, one from herself and one, written with her left hand, from an anonymous, mysterious admirer, the same one who sent him a Valentine every year.

June was sure that Eddie would never win a fist fight, never have a good job and never receive a Valentine from anyone other than his grandmother. And it would all be her fault somehow. She imagined him when she was dead – a solitary middle-aged man ('pleasant enough') living in a stained and soiled flat, obsessively collecting newspapers and cereal packets.

The American flagfish – *Jordanella floridae*. A good name for a girl, Eddie thought. 'Oh yes, and may I introduce my girlfriend, Miss Jordanella Floridae?' He chortled. His nearly adolescent antennae sensed his mother watching disapprovingly from the doorway and he deliberately picked his nose to annoy her. He was looking forward to having a girlfriend, he knew he'd end up with a geeky one but he didn't mind. They'd be pals, the way he was going to be pals with his invisible sister.

June regarded Eddie with despair. He was sitting cross-legged in the middle of the carpet, bent almost double over an old book and cackling manically to himself. The new baby fluttered inside her, elbowing more room for itself. June wanted to tell Eddie that she loved him but instead she said, 'Don't pick your nose, Eddie.'

'Do I look like my father?' he asked when she had already left the room. 'I can't remember what he looked like,' she shouted from the hallway. Which was more or less true. He didn't often ask but when he did she always said his father was 'some guy she met on holiday'. Which was also more or less true.

'What do you want to do for your birthday, squirt?' Hawk asked. Hawk was staring at the table in front of him on which the innards of a barometer, acquired at a car boot sale, were laid out in a way that suggested they would never go back together again.

'Deep Sea World,' Eddie replied instantly.

'Again?'

'Again.'

'Oh, not again.' June sighed as they headed out across the Forth Road Bridge in Hawk's tinny old van. She was doing her best, but she felt sick. 'It's the fourth time this year, Eddie.'

'It's *my* birthday, I get to choose,' Eddie said cheerfully.

'We could have gone to Butterfly World,' June said, more to herself than anyone. The baby would like Butterfly World. A girl who would like butterflies. Hawk's van smelt of wet dog as they drove across the Forth Road Bridge, the water grey beneath their wheels.

June didn't like the sea. She had done once but not after Crete. It had been her first holiday abroad – her parents had never been comfortable with the idea of foreign holidays, they contained too many potential hazards. There were four of them – two boys, Andy and Mark, herself and a girl called Joanna, who was a midwife now (June had seen her at the antenatal clinic), which you would never have thought would be her fate if you'd met her then.

They had taken a little boat out onto that vast expanse of azure as different from the Firth of Forth as was possible and when they were a long way from shore they all decided to go swimming off the boat. They'd been drinking retsina and smoking dope after a big lunch of oily moussaka and green beans (her father would have said they were going out of their way to die) but they were all reckless, or maybe they all thought they were immortal. June wasn't sure that she thought at all at that age.

June was a strong swimmer – her parents had made sure she could swim as drowning was always high on their list of likely ways to die – and she had loved the feeling of kicking out in all that warm water with the sun like a bronze mirror in the sky, beating down on her back. They had seen flying silver fish and a school of dolphins before they dived in the water and June was hoping that one of the dolphins would come back and find her. She had seen a mosaic once, in some Roman villa on one of the sunless British holidays her parents took her on, and in the mosaic a boy was riding on a dolphin's back, and June thought if she could do that, if she could ride on a dolphin, she would be happy. And if she could actually turn into a dolphin, then she might be happy for ever.

At first she thought that maybe it was a dolphin that took her down because, without any warning, she found herself being dragged abruptly to the bottom of the Mediterranean. Straight down, not the floundering, bubbling chaos of cramp or tiredness, but a speeding, rushing drop as if an anchor had been tied to her feet. And the odd thing was, when she arrived on the seabed, stepping lightly off the rock she had landed on as if getting off a bus, she could still breathe.

She could remember seeing shells and fish, squid and crabs, she could remember the sunlight on the surface, a long way above her head. She could even remember how it felt to glide as effortlessly as a water nymph through the sea, but after that everything was confused in her memory and what happened next was so very rich and strange that she thought that someone must have given her acid. Certainly dropping acid was the only logical explanation she could come up with afterwards for the underwater kingdom – the massive throne of green marble decorated with gold and red coral and mother-of-pearl and cushioned with sealskin, the sea beasts that swam around like lap dogs, the massive white horses whose manes were huge waves endlessly breaking around their heads as they pawed the sand, impatient to be harnessed to his chariot. And only some serious psychotropic drug could have accounted for his colossal, roaring presence of which she seemed only to catch fragments – the disgusting smell of fish and whale fat, the fronds of seaweed entangled in his great beard, his seed like pearls, gushing into the blue water—

'You all right?' Hawk asked her.

'Fine,' June said.

'What shall we call the baby?' Eddie asked from the back of the van and June's heart gave a little flap at the word 'we'. June and Eddie. June and Eddie and the baby. A family. She wanted to squash Eddie to her breast. Instead she said, 'Close your mouth, Eddie. If the wind changes you'll stay like that.'

June knew that Eddie liked everything in Deep Sea World but that the thing he liked most was the Underwater Safari – the moving walkway in the huge acrylic-that-looked-like-glass tunnel that took you down, down, right into the kingdom of fishes, from the forests of sunlit kelp where the little fish darted, to the sandy flats where the skate hid on the bottom, to the depths of the abyss where the scary conger eels lurked, to the open ocean with its shimmering silver fish. June was convinced that the weight of the water would break the tunnel and they would all be swept away on a North Sea tsunami of cod and salmon and sea bass. She reminded herself to think happy thoughts for the sake of the baby.

Someone called Jamie had a birthday today. Eddie knew that because there was a handwritten sign stuck up in the tunnel amongst the seaweed fronds, a sign that said 'Happy Seventh Birthday, Jamie'. Eddie didn't suppose anyone had done the same for him but that didn't stop him hoping.

'Shite,' June said when she saw the happy birthday sign. 'Shite, shite, shite.' Why didn't she know you could do that? Because she was a crap mother, obviously. She imagined how happy Eddie would have been if he'd had a sign. She felt sick again.

Afterwards, they ate in the cafeteria, an indifferent meal of chips and baked beans because it seemed wrong to eat fish. It was wet and windy outside and so cold that for once Hawk's van felt warm. June wanted a cigarette. Surely the baby wouldn't mind just one cigarette?

Going home, they got stuck halfway across the bridge in a rush-hour traffic jam. Hawk drummed a tuneless tune on the steering wheel. The water beneath was a wretched steel colour with a curdled froth on the wind-whipped waves. June wondered how long they would survive in the water if the suspension cables snapped.

Eddie had his nose pressed to the back window of the van. The rain had cleared behind them, bathing Fife in a watery gold sun. Down in the water Eddie could see mermaids leaping out of the river like salmon, their goldfish tails catching the sun. Nereids sunbathed on Inchcolm Island while a huge shoal of silver fish whirled the Forth into a vortex in obeisance to their secret god – Eddie, King of the Fish. 'Thank you, loyal subjects,' Eddie said, giving a regal wave to the inhabitants of his watery realm.

'Don't talk to yourself, Eddie,' June said. 'It's the first sign of madness.'

June wondered if Hawk would hang around long enough to see the baby born. She wished he would leave now instead of putting her through the misery of waiting for him to go. Hawk himself was thinking that he fancied joining a tepee community. The baby inside June wasn't thinking at all, it was leaping for the joy of leaping.

Eddie laughed to himself because he, and only he, knew

what the great blue and white marbled carp had said to him that day in the Botanics.

Eddie leant forward and put his small, hot, dirty hand into June's hand and said, 'Everything's going to be OK, Mum. Trust me.'

III

TRANSPARENT FICTION

Exultation is the going
Of an inland soul to sea,
Past the houses, past the headlands,
Into deep eternity.

EMILY DICKINSON

EREDITH ZANE, TWENTY-FIVE-YEAR-OLD PHARMAcology post-grad from California, was working her way round Europe between finishing her doctorate and taking up a junior teaching post at MIT. Meredith was a goal-orientated sort of girl who thrived on purposes and objectives. She always had a just-washed look about her and was a preppy, patriotic dresser – Ralph Lauren and Calvin Klein mainly, a little Hilfiger. She never wore black clothes or red lipstick. Her hair was pulled neatly back in a ponytail and she had travelled through her life so far in sensible flats and sneakers. She had been using both contraception and recreational drugs since she was sixteen but had never let either sex or mind-altering substances interfere with her progress. Untroubled by death or history or love, Meredith was, in short, an all-American girl.

These latter omissions – love, history, death – would, she

presumed, be rectified during the course of her Grand Tour of Europe. She prepared herself in the travel section of Borders, curled up on an overstuffed, overused sofa, surrounded by maps and guidebooks, plotting an itinerary that would take her to places the very names of which swooned with decadence – Paris, Venice, Lisbon, Seville, Naples, Siena, Vienna. Meredith's emigrant blood was stirred by the idea of regaining entrance to the museum of Europe and raking over its musty contents in cathedrals and chateaux, temples and amphitheatres, where the air would be thick with the fine dust of the dead.

Four months later and she was still in England, or London, to be more precise. The only other part of England she had seen was Middlesbrough, a godforsaken, *Blade Runner* kind of place, to which she had travelled with Fletcher for his grandmother's funeral.

Meredith had moved in with Fletcher three days after landing at Heathrow, more as a matter of convenience than commitment – Fletcher wasn't the kind of guy to base any sort of life decision on. For one, he was English, and for two, he had an insecure streak as wide as a six-lane blacktop. Meredith was fond of Fletcher but in much the same way she'd been fond of Chip, a Golden Retriever that had been her childhood's constant companion.

Meredith had gone through life borrowing other people's personalities rather than going to the trouble of developing her own. She found it was a good way of avoiding the anguished introspection that most people seemed prey to. Meredith's own family provided a vast assortment of personae from which she could pick and mix. For example, if she had to lead a tricky seminar she adopted the calm, authoritative personality of her own mother, Anna, a renowned paediatrician. For an altercation, in a store, say, over substandard goods, Meredith looked to her cousin Wilson, who was in such a permanent bad mood that it seemed as if she was allergic to life.

For her current job – working in a Knightsbridge department store on a floor that sold accessories – Meredith adopted the serene yet worldly personality of her mother's sister Jenna. Jenna ran an interior design company in Los Angeles where she worked almost entirely from a palette of neutral colours. She had once, famously, painted a movie star's house in ten shades of white, only five of which were discernible to the naked eye. The client loved it. In this spirit, Meredith urged Fendi baguettes and Georgina von Etzdorf scarves onto customers who felt strangely flattered by the seriousness of her attentions.

For her relationship with Fletcher, Meredith usually looked to the perky, cheerleading qualities of her cousin Baxter. Baxter, a beauty-pageant veteran by the age of seven, had, in turn, based her own character on that of her 'Air Stewardess' Barbie. Fletcher responded well to this purloined personality. Meredith knew that most men would rather have Air Stewardess Barbie in bed with them than a girl with a doctoral thesis entitled 'The conservation of telomere length in the human myocardium: the role of telomerase reverse transcriptase'.

Fletcher was a writer on the television soap *Green Acres*, a long-running, low-expectations kind of show. Meredith had never understood the attraction of soaps. Her cousin Tyler, an aficionado of daytime television, had often tried, to no effect, to tutor Meredith in the kitsch value of *Melrose Place* or *The Bold and the Beautiful*, but then Tyler was a performance artist in New York and therefore, by definition, completely flaky (which was, Meredith had discovered late one night returning from a party, a good personality to adopt if you wanted to avoid a ticket from a speed cop). Not that *Green Acres* bore any relation to its transatlantic colleagues – on *Green Acres* it was big news if a sheep crossed the road. Fletcher said he was waiting for something better to come up. Meanwhile, he put in a couple of days a week on *Green Acres* and spent the rest of the time watching *Buffy* on video, playing Gran Turismo on his PlayStation or listening to alternative country songs about road kill and suicide.

If she'd been back in the States, Meredith wouldn't have given Fletcher the time of day. But she wasn't back in the States, she was in Europe – even if it was only England – and therefore she accepted, even embraced, a certain lowering of her standards.

Meredith thought of herself as a tourist in Fletcher's life. Tourism was in the blood of the Zanes. They had been inclined to nomadic behaviour as long as anyone could remember. The first Zane had come to America from Poland way back when the Zanes were still Zanowskis. The Zanowskis were pedlars back then – ribbons and fabric and trimmings – working their way west with the frontier. The Zanes spread out across the newfound land like bison on the prairie. When they reached Chicago the Zanowskis transformed themselves into the less unwieldy 'Zanes' and opened a five-floor department store. Other Zanes continued to roll the frontier back, pushing it all the way to the Pacific where Meredith's mother, Anna Zane, was born in Sacramento. Anna and her six younger sisters – Jenna, Tania, Vari, Debbi, Cara and Nanci, all born after the war to an orthodontist and a housewife – were turned out on a domestic assembly-line that could have rivalled Ford. The Zane sisters, as they were known in those American dream-days, were the very best their country could produce. Their dairy-enriched bones were strong, their meatloaf-and-spinach-fed muscles were supple and their vitamin-nourished brains got them all into the top ten percentiles of their school classes – all except for Debbi who was more of the homecoming-queen type and who married – disastrously – her high-school sweetheart (Baxter, the beauty-pageant princess, was her eldest).

The Zane sisters' dental work was carried out by their father, the orthodontist, so they all had great teeth and could smile for America, all except for Vari who had a jumbled mouthful of molars that just wouldn't straighten out – something that mystified her father right up to the day he shot himself.

After the frontier fell into the sea, there was nowhere else for the more pioneering of the Zanes to go except back from where they came – to the cold, old world. This journey was not always a matter of choice. Henry Zane, for instance (one of the Idaho Zanes), went to Belgium in 1918 as a reluctant infantryman, and never came back, dying in the influenza pandemic. Nor did Wesley (a Minneapolis Zane) return to the new world. He just managed to put a foot on French soil in 1944 – or, more correctly, French sand – before being blown up on Omaha beach. Before Henry and Wesley, the trail had been blazed by a considerably more willing Adelaide Zane, heiress to the Chicago department store fortune. Adelaide met and married a penniless Italian count while she was on the Grand Tour. Adelaide died in childbirth at the end of her first year of marriage and the Italian count inherited her fortune and disappeared into history. There was a tendency amongst some Zanes to think of Adelaide as a doomed, romantic figure, but in truth, she was a plain girl with a fondness for small dogs and liquorice and her count was no Gilbert Osmond. Adelaide and her baby, the first Zane to be born in the old world since 1801, were buried together in a churchyard in Florence.

One of the European tasks that Meredith had given

herself before leaving California was to discover the graves of all these mortally expatriate Zanes and yet now the energy for that, or indeed for any other task, seemed to have all but disappeared. From almost the moment her American Airlines plane had touched down on English tarmac, Meredith had succumbed to an odd malaise, a mysterious kind of inertia that lay on her like a fog. She suspected she was suffering from an overabundance of history, something she'd never had to deal with in California. Or perhaps it was just the stale and sickly air that circulated and recirculated above the streets of London, leaving her lungs feeling like wrung-out cloths so that sometimes at night she would be woken by the sensation that a heavy weight, like a very large cat, had made itself comfortable on her chest while she was asleep and pressed all the air out of her. She would wake with a start, gasping like a newly caught fish, and lie awake for the rest of the night, lost in a strange miasma of doubt and dispiritedness. She worried that this might be her true character.

Her cousin Tyler, the performance artist, was the only person Meredith had bothered to tell about Fletcher. It was such a temporary liaison that there seemed no point in worrying her mother and her aunts back home with it. They believed that any Zane who went to Europe was pretty much doomed, but marrying a foreigner more or less sealed your fate. The youngest of the Zane sisters, Nanci, had been the last Zane to succumb to the European curse. Nanci had undertaken her own Grand Tour in the seventies. England was her last port of call, in all senses of the word. She married an English guy whose name Meredith had forgotten and died under anaesthetic in a dentist's surgery in London. Nanci was just twenty-five when she died – the same age as Meredith was now.

Meredith didn't need to worry about tracking down Nanci's grave. Nanci had mouldered in a drier climate back in Sacramento – the Zanes flew her body home after her sudden check-out and she was buried next to her father, who had blown his brains out when he heard his baby had died at the hands of another dentist. Family legend had it that Nanci was missing a finger when she arrived back in California.

Those Zane sisters were now the Zane aunts, and all of them, apart from the dead Nanci, had produced children. Even Jenna, who was gay, had improved the Zane gene pool by going to a sperm donor centre and buying the milt of a Boston neurosurgeon to make three daughters. An impoverished Korean concert pianist had provided the anonymous means for a fourth after Jenna grew bored with her progressively scientific spawn.

Fletcher was not the first male to be puzzled by the extraordinary preponderance of female Zanes, made more baffling by the fact that all of Meredith's generation seemed to have boys' names. Meredith, Baxter and Wilson – which sounded like a firm of lawyers – were all girls, as were the endlessly confusing Taylor, Tyler, Skyler and Sky. Sydney and Jeri were sisters. Sky had sisters Storm and Summer (all three were offspring of Vari, who had taken an alternative path in the sixties). For a long time, Fletcher presumed that Meredith's brother Bradley must be a girl. 'Well, he almost is,' Meredith said. Apparently, Bradley had also used Baxter's Air Stewardess Barbie as a role model.

None of the Zanes was Christian (apart from Debbi who was born again – twice) and certainly not Catholic, yet they seemed to go in for unfashionably large families. Fletcher wondered if they were trying to upset the gender balance by breeding nothing but girls. Men seemed dispensable to the Zane women. Fletcher suspected that their true goal was probably autogenesis – replicating themselves endlessly like a fractal, a Zane fractal. According to Meredith, her cousins were all either lesbians (Wilson, Taylor), virgins (Baxter, Sky) or – a considerably longer list – promiscuous (Tyler, Skyler, Sydney, Storm, Summer, Jeri and Meredith).

'But you're not promiscuous,' Fletcher said to Meredith, more in optimism than in protest.

'Not right this minute,' Meredith agreed (an unsatisfactory answer at best).

Nor was Fletcher the first man to fall prey to an obsession with the Zane girls, a kind of Zaneitis, like an infection of the brain, so that he often found himself wondering what Sky was doing, who Jeri was with, what Tyler was wearing. He had never met any of these Zane cousins, of course, he'd never even seen a photograph, he just presumed they all looked exactly like Meredith. In his more paranoid moments, usually when he'd smoked too much dope, Fletcher found himself considering the possibility that the Zanes might actually be some form of extraterrestrial invasion. This would explain why they had such large families – broadcasting their alien seed so that eventually everyone on the planet would be Zane clones, all blond and blue-eyed like the children in *Village of the Damned*.

'Would it help allay your insane fears if I told you that Sky and Storm were redheads and that Harry was fat?' Meredith offered.

'No,' Fletcher said, 'it wouldn't.'

Meredith woke with a start, unable to breathe, her heart stopped for a beat. When it started again, it was wild and fluttering like a small bird that had just escaped great danger. The clock on the bedside table said 3.30. That was when most people died, she knew. By the negative light of the moon, Fletcher looked as pale as a sleeping vampire by her side.

Meredith wondered what would happen to her if she remained in London. Would the low level of oxygen affect her longevity? Stop her heart for ever, before she'd had time to live her life, like poor Nanci and Adelaide before her?

What if she, too, was a mere sideshoot of the Zane family tree? Meredith experienced a small, unaccustomed thrill of fear at this thought. What if she were to succumb to the curse the old world had laid on the Zanes, what if she were to fly home from her Grand Tour in the cargo bay of a 747, possibly minus a finger? Or worse.

Meredith thought about the cells in her body slowly, invisibly dying, life never to be replaced. Meredith knew what mortality was, it was her speciality. No, not mortality, she silently corrected herself, her subject was immortality. Sometimes she tried to talk to Fletcher about her research. 'Telomeres,' she would explain hopefully, 'the physical ends of our chromosomes, nucleoprotein complexes that help to protect and reproduce chromosomes. The longer our telomeres, the longer we live.' But he would frown in the way he did when he was forced to do mental arithmetic. 'Think of it,' she persisted, trying to find an analogy simple enough for him, 'like the caps on the ends of sneaker laces, that stop them fraying.'

Meredith couldn't sleep. She thought about her telomeres shortening each time a cell divided, like little Doomsday clocks, counting out her cells' days, shorter and shorter, counting out her body's life, heartbeat by heartbeat, and was still awake when Selene drove her exhausted horses, gleaming with silvery sweat, the last few paces of the night.

*

Meredith planned to sneak away, to slip out of the door in the middle of the night while Fletcher was asleep. She bought her tickets, handed in her notice at the department store, collected her dry cleaning and studied her maps. She shot a whole roll of film of Fletcher so that when she went home she'd be able to show people the guy she lived with in London. She could imagine herself saying, 'Yeah, he was a writer,' and her friends saying, 'Cool.'

Meredith was due to fly to Paris on Saturday morning. On the Friday she discovered the key to eternal life. This was how it happened. Meredith came home from her last day working in the department store, her head still full of pashminas and tiny jewelled bags, and found Fletcher staring wild-eyed at his computer screen. His desk was littered with empty yoghurt cartons and overflowing ash-trays and on the stereo a country band was singing about the back roads of Texas in a way that made Meredith want to shoot out the speakers.

'I'm trying to get this finished,' Fletcher said, typing with one hand while lighting a cigarette with the other, 'so I can take it with me tonight to show Fiddy Ross.'

'Fiddy Ross?' Meredith repeated vaguely.

'Yes, Fiddy Ross.' Fletcher frowned impatiently at her. 'The television producer? The television producer who has invited us round to her house for dinner tonight. A dinner party,' he added unnecessarily, enunciating as if speaking to a foreigner. Which he was, Meredith supposed.

'OK,' she said, acquiescing in an easy Baxterish kind of way out of respect for the fact that this was the man she was planning to abandon without a backward glance the following day.

Fletcher jabbed a nicotine-stained finger at the computer screen. 'It's the treatment for a TV screenplay,' he said, 'a kind of historical-medical-detective thing, sort of *Silent Witness* meets *The House of Eliott*. I'm going to give it to Fiddy Ross tonight.'

'Is that wise?' Meredith asked.

'Wise?' Fletcher repeated as if the word was slightly beyond his reach.

'Well, it's just a social occasion.'

'They're *television* people,' Fletcher said, 'nothing's "just" a social occasion for them.'

Meredith and Fletcher had arrived late and breathless at Fiddy Ross's front door after being stuck on the tube. It was an unpleasantly humid night, sullen thunder grumbling and rolling around the sky above Primrose Hill. The front door was opened by a gloomy girl who greeted them suspiciously. 'The guests are all here,' she said truculently when Fletcher mentioned his name. Indifference finally got the better of her and she let them in.

It wasn't what Meredith would have called a dinner party. A dinner party was something her mother used to throw, before her father left, of course, before her father left to live on a boat in Florida with a Cuban lap dancer. Before her divorce, which she had handled very badly, Anna Zane had done everything well throughout her life, including dinner parties, using recipes from Julia Child's *Mastering the Art of French Cooking*, which impressed even the relatively sophisticated palates of the Sacramento professionals who were the guests at her table. Fiddy Ross's idea of a dinner party, on the other hand, was a much more ad hoc affair, a buffet which had clearly been purchased in Marks and Spencer's food hall and laid out in the kitchen, a space too small for all the people crowded into it. The food was already congealing unattractively in the overheated atmosphere. People were eating and talking simultaneously, like overly conversational vultures, the food sometimes falling out of their mouths in their eagerness to talk.

Fletcher and Meredith stood awkwardly in the doorway like shy creatures arriving late at a waterhole. Fiddy, for Meredith presumed it must be her, suddenly spotted them and rushed over as if they were masked intruders, her features fixed in an interrogative spasm.

'Fletcher,' Fletcher said, 'Fletcher Smith. We met at the *Queer Street* screening. You invited me tonight. You did,' he added helpfully as Fiddy twisted her neck and turned her face up like a thoughtful flamingo in order to access her memory. Fiddy had strange hair, dyed a kind of magenta colour and cropped in a spiky, close cut that belonged on a much younger woman.

'Yes!' she said suddenly so that Meredith flinched, 'yes, of course, I'm so sorry, really the most appalling memory. Everyone,' she clapped her hands like a primary school teacher, 'this is Fletcher and . . . ?' Fiddy seemed to see Meredith for the first time.

'Meredith,' Meredith said. 'Meredith Zane.' None of Fiddy's guests paid any attention to this introduction, except for one, a man standing near them, shaped like a bowling ball. 'Zane,' he boomed in an American accent. 'Did you say Zane? No relation to Monty Zane, used to be with Paramount? From Atlanta originally, I believe.'

'The Georgia Zanes,' Meredith shrugged. 'There were a lot of them.'

The bowling-ball guy was smoking a cigar after the fashion of a cartoon tycoon. He stuck out his surprisingly small, square hand. 'Lester,' he said. 'Lester Goldman.' Meredith shook the hand, aware of a strange choking noise coming from Fletcher by her side. '*The* Lester Goldman?' he managed to say. Whereas others might have modestly demurred that there were surely other Lester Goldmans in the world, this Lester Goldman merely said, 'Yeah, *the* Lester Goldman.'

'The biggest film producer in the world,' Fletcher murmured, almost faint with happiness, like a man who had just been shown the small, secret, side door through which he might gain entrance to heaven. Meredith left him to it.

Ignoring the increasingly unattractive food, she poured

herself a glass of wine and attempted to mingle with the other guests. No easy task as even before she had introduced herself their eyes were roaming round the room looking for someone more interesting.

The number of people in the kitchen seemed to have doubled. Although most of them appeared to be media people of one kind or another, they nearly all seemed to have problems communicating. A very tall, very black girl who looked like a model was refusing to talk to anyone, not just Meredith. Fiddy's PA, a Spanish woman called Paula, was speaking incomprehensible English, apparently giving out orders to people, and growing increasingly angry when no one obeyed. A producer called Will, a boyish lazy-looking sort, was having a furious, sotto voce argument with his girlfriend Masha, the gloomy girl (even gloomier now) who had opened the door to them. Fiddy herself moved amongst her guests like a queen while people cooed ridiculously flattering things at her. 'You are clever, Fiddy, all this lovely food. Just like Nigella.'

Occasionally Meredith would check on how Fletcher was doing with Lester Goldman. Each time she looked Lester was chewing on his cigar while Fletcher pitched and tossed plots at him like a lunatic putting on a one-man show. Looking at Fletcher amongst all these people she felt an odd twitch in her heart, not so much love as fear.

Someone claiming to be Fiddy's husband splashed more wine into Meredith's glass. He was called something dog-like and monosyllabic that Meredith immediately forgot (Sam? Max?) and tried to manoeuvre her out into the conservatory, apparently with the intention of having sex with her amongst the desiccated maidenhair ferns, and was only discouraged from this albeit rather half-hearted pursuit by being suddenly attacked by three small children. 'Ankle-biters,' he snarled at them and shouted for the nanny. This nanny (the oddly named Missy) efficiently marshalled the children and steered them out of the conservatory, although not before giving Fiddy's husband a disparaging look as if he was a particularly badly behaved five-year-old boy.

'Arietty, Hugo and little Nell,' he said to Meredith, once Missy had gone, 'fantastic kids.'

Fiddy's husband spotted someone important foraging at the buffet table and made a hasty exit. Meredith sat down on a rusted cast-iron chair. For the first time in her life she wanted a cigarette. She couldn't wait to get out of this town, out of this deadbeat country. Slowly, like something tugging at her consciousness, she grew aware that she was not alone in the conservatory. In a corner, half hidden by a limp and unfruitful grapevine, a woman was sitting in a chair, one of those big basket ones with a peacock back, so that the imperial impression she gave was reinforced. With her lacquered black hair arranged in an intricate style, her rouge-reddened cheeks and her beady black eyes, she had the air of a Chinese dowager empress.

The woman was dressed in a very peculiar fashion, even

for this part of London – a cocktail dress in an emerald raw silk that looked as if it dated from the early sixties, and over it the oddest garment that Meredith had ever seen. It was not so much a cloak as a cape and was made from some weird material. From a distance it looked like feathers, iridescent green, plucked from hundreds of small birds or butterflies, yet, closer to, the feathers seemed more like scales – an exotic lizard or an Amazonian snake. The odd thing was that the more Meredith looked at them the more difficult they were to see.

'Merle,' this lamian figure said, in a low, almost guttural voice, 'Merle Goldman, Lester's wife.' She extended a hand, which Meredith took reluctantly. The skin on Merle Goldman's face was stretched tautly across the bones, shiny and papery, as if she'd undergone a hundred facelifts. But when she lifted her hand to shake Meredith's and the sleeve of the emerald dress fell away, she revealed an ancient arm, brownish and simian, striated with wrinkles and splashed with liver spots. Meredith was reminded of a photograph she had once seen of a mummified Inca sacrifice. She felt Merle's red talons scratching her skin as they shook hands and smelt her breath with its strange scent – sickly sweet like embalming fluid. Meredith found old people disturbing even at a distance, but close up she felt that she could not only see the skull beneath Merle Goldman's skin, but also the ropy sinews, the leaky blood vessels, the lamp-black lungs, the creaky ancient pump of a heart. She gave a little shiver of horror and Merle croaked with laughter. 'You think *you'll* live for ever, honey?'

It was odd because Meredith was sure that she had spent no more than a few minutes with Merle in Fiddy Ross's conservatory and yet afterwards she was left with the impression that she had spent hours listening to an outlandish fiction that Merle Goldman claimed to be her life story, a tale which afterwards would disintegrate into a thousand and one half-forgotten shards that Meredith could not piece together again no matter how hard she tried. All she knew was that Merle's life had begun a long time ago somewhere in the Mediterranean and had traversed centuries of time and taken in tombs as gorgeous as palaces, palaces as grand as kingdoms, and involved intrigues and exiles, revolutions and wars, sealed trains across continents and sleigh journeys wrapped in wolfskins, and had somehow or other ended up in Hollywood (which was probably the appropriate place for it in Meredith's opinion) and marriage to Lester Goldman.

The foetid atmosphere of the conservatory and the endlessly woven fabric of Merle's tale had left Meredith feeling sick and flushed as if she had been slumped in some opiated dream. She was relieved when Lester barrelled up, a deliriously happy Fletcher in tow.

'Honey,' Lester said solicitously to his wife, 'we should be heading back to the hotel, you've gotta get your beauty sleep.'

And that was when it happened. As Lester Goldman helped his wife up from her peacock throne, Merle's extraordinary reptilian cape slipped so that her withered shoulders were exposed to the air. In that instant she began to disintegrate – the skin turning to dust, the flesh liquefying and melting, and, for a fragment of a second, as if in some unearthly X-ray, Meredith really did see the skeleton beneath Merle's skin. She wanted to turn to Fletcher and say, 'Wow, just like the vampires in *Buffy* when they're staked,' but she couldn't move, and anyway Lester and Fletcher had failed to witness this extraordinary event and had begun an animated conversation about some witness protection plot that was a perfect vehicle for Jodie Foster. Merle had moved as fast as a snake to grab the cape and replace it, holding it close at her throat as if she was freezing cold.

Meredith looked into Merle Goldman's eyes. Meredith Zane's blue, all-American-girl eyes looked deep into Merle Goldman's glittering old European eyes and a cold horror should have gripped her heart. But it didn't.

'Lester,' Merle said hoarsely, 'time to go, lamb chop.'

A car and a uniformed driver were waiting for the Goldmans on the pavement outside Fiddy Ross's house. Fiddy was nowhere in sight so it was Fletcher and Meredith who performed the hostess's duty of farewells. The driver opened the door of the car for Merle. Meredith could see her scarlet nails digging into the sleeve of Lester's unimaginably expensive suit as she positioned herself to get into the back seat.

Meredith knew what she had to do. Without daring to breathe, without daring to think, Meredith snatched at the cape, grabbing it as hard as she could with both hands and hauling it off Merle Goldman's body. She heard Merle give an unearthly shriek and she heard Lester say, 'Jesus Christ, what the fuck is going on?' and she caught a glimpse of Fletcher's disbelieving, ashen face as Merle crumbled into dust in front of his eyes and finally – and not before time, in Meredith's opinion – joined the massed ranks of the dead.

In her purse she had a plane ticket and an American Express card. On her feet she had a pair of Air Max Motos that were already eating up the grey, gum-stuck pavements of London. Her hair fell free from its band and streamed in her wake. Thunder cracked overhead. Meredith threw the cape over her shoulders. It felt impossibly beautiful. Meredith laughed as she ran, neatly side-stepping the golden apples lying in her path. She carried on running and running. Meredith Zane ran into the future for ever.

IV

DISSONANCE

Beareth all things, believeth all things, hopeth all things, endureth all things.

ST PAUL, I CORINTHIANS, 13:7

For Maureen Allan

SIMON WISHED HIS MOTHER WOULD DIE. RIGHT THAT minute. Right where she was sitting, which was almost undoubtedly down in the kitchen, at the bloody kitchen table, doing her bloody marking. *I'm at my wits' end with you, Simon. I worry about what's going to happen to you, I really do.* Well, if she was dead she wouldn't have to worry, would she? And he wouldn't have to listen to her bloody nagging. *Shoes don't live in the kitchen, Simon. If you spill something, do you think you could wipe it up, Simon? Do you know what a dishwasher's for, Simon?* He knew what would go on her bloody headstone as well. *I've just cleaned that, Simon.*

Korn's *Life is Peachy* pounded on the stereo, helping keep his thoughts in rhythm with Tekken 3 on the PlayStation. Hwoarang hammered machine-gun punches into Lei Wulong's stomach *Simon, if you're going to finish all the milk, could you buy more?* Paul Phoenix pulled a three-hit combo with a God Hammer punch on Yoshimitsu *If you use something, could you put it back when you've finished with it, Simon?* Simon snorted with adolescent schadenfreude as he imagined his mother in the King of the Iron Fists tournament, Forest Law thwacking junkyard kicks into her virtual body parts, Jin Kazama chopping her into submission *Do you remember when you used to kiss and cuddle me and call me 'Mummy'?*

She was going to tell his father. *Shoplifting, Simon. That's theft, pure and simple.* Like the shops weren't ripping him off in the first place. *And how do you work that one out, Simon?* She knew he couldn't argue like Rebecca. She was always trying to get him to explain things. *Why did you do that, Simon? What were you thinking?* Stupid cow. *Just because your father doesn't live with us any more doesn't mean he can abdicate his responsibilities.* 'Tell Dad if you want, I haven't even seen him in weeks.' Dad wasn't interested in them any more anyway. He had Jenny now. *It'll never last.* Jenny who was pregnant, except their mother didn't know it. *What do you think will happen to you if you keep on this path, Simon? Hm?* King punched Ling Xiaoyu and then jumped on her body. KO. Ling Xiaoyu gave a girly little scream. Game Over. You Win.

Rebecca was making a bar chart for Higher Maths to the untroubling sound of Travis on her headphones. She was using Excel – neat blocks of red, blue, green and purple that would come out nicely on her Epson colour printer.

Rebecca liked everything to be neat. Her room was completely coordinated – lilacs, purples and blues, a touch of pink but not too girly. She didn't think of herself as a girly girl. The cover on her bed was pulled smooth, her books and files aligned with the edge of her shelf. *You take after your father, don't you?*

She checked the clock. 21.43. At ten o'clock she'd make hot chocolate. Rebecca thought she might buy a kettle and a small microwave for her bedroom. She had enough money, she'd worked as soon as she could get a job – down at the Alldays, in the video shop – now she worked in Superdrug on Saturdays and holidays. Her own money, not guilty paternal handouts. *You're so self-sufficient, Rebecca.* If she had a microwave and a kettle she'd never have to bother with the rest of the house, apart from the bathroom. It was a shame her Superdrug job didn't run to funding an en-suite bathroom, then she could just stay in her own neat nest. She couldn't wait to be living in a hall of residence.

22.00. Rebecca removed her headphones and was assaulted by the noise from Simon's stereo. No wonder he had mince for brains. And he played such shite. Korn, for Christ's sake. *I don't know, when I was your age songs used to have a tune.* When their mother came out with her nostalgia crap Rebecca felt the same irritation as her brother but she would never give him the pleasure of sibling camaraderie by telling him that. Their mother talked about her youth a lot these days, ever since Beardy Brian came on the scene. They used to be at university together, a fact that seemed to continually amaze them both – *Who'd have thought then that we'd get together?* – as if they were the only two Aberdeen university alumni on the planet.

'Alumni'. That was a word she had learnt from Beardy Brian. She'd tucked it away for further use. 'Yes, I'm a Trinity alumnus.' They did Latin at Watson's, she knew her plurals. Their mother never stopped telling them how lucky they were to do Latin. *In my day everyone did it. Now you only get taught it if you go to expensive schools like yours. What about my poor kids, don't they deserve the choice?* But they had never had Latin on the curriculum at the schemie school her mother taught at and she knew it.

Not that Rebecca was sure about Cambridge. There were plenty of places she could apply to. *But Edinburgh has an excellent reputation for medicine – then you could live at home.* Yeah, that'll be right.

Not that she was entirely sure about medicine either. Her subjects were strong across the board, maybe she should do an Arts degree. But when she thought of herself in the future – which was all the time – she saw herself as a doctor, not in some scummy NHS hospital but as a surgeon with Médecins sans Frontières, operating in impossible conditions in a war zone, or a doctor in some remote mountain village vaccinating the photogenic babies of noble tribeswomen. Dr Rebecca McFarlane.

Rebecca opened Simon's door and yelled at him to turn

his stereo down. His face flushed a furious fuchsia at this intrusion.

'You wouldn't stand for it if I came into your room without knocking, would you?'

'No, I'd fucking kill you,' she said matter-of-factly. It was hard to believe anyone she shared so many genes with could be so unattractive. Simon had spots like Braille. A blind person could probably read half of Shakespeare on his face. 'It stinks in here, Simon.'

'Leave then.'

'No, really. I'm serious, it's disgusting.'

You do shower every day, don't you, Simon?

'I said leave.'

'You shouldn't wank so much in here.'

She managed to close the door just in time for his trainer to thud off it. 'Whore,' he yelled as Rebecca ran lightly down the stairs, laughing.

Their mother was standing at the kitchen door, a frown contracting her round moon features, her voice full of concern. *Did he just call you a whore, Becca?* 'Yeah, you'd better go and throw *The Female Eunuch* at him.' *You can't call women whores, even if you don't mean it.* 'But what about if they actually are whores?' *It's a derogatory term. Language is how we define our world.* 'Yeah, use that argument on Simon, why don't you, like he'll really understand what you're talking about.'

Her mother was wearing that disgusting, worn-out denim smock that looked as if she'd had it since she was pregnant.

She looked pregnant in it now. She had no waistline whatsoever. She took her glasses off and let them dangle on the chain which bounced off her cushiony breasts as she walked up the stairs. She might as well not be wearing a bra.

Her mother's underwear was horrible, everything slightly grey and stretched, the elastic gone in the M and S sports bras she wore, even though she was the least sporty person Rebecca could think of. Rebecca did her own washing. The idea of contaminating anything she wore with her mother's saggy bras and washed-to-death Sloggis or – infinitely worse – Simon's skid-marked, urine-spotted boxers, *At least make an effort to aim for the toilet bowl, Simon*, made her feel ill.

Rebecca's underwear was spotlessly white – she pre-soaked it in Vanish – she preferred white and so, luckily, did her boyfriend, Fraser. Fraser was as good as they got, captain of the rugby team and Dux of the school, he had his own car and was allowed to have Rebecca to stay whenever he wanted, although they never had sex in his house, Rebecca couldn't bear the idea of Fraser's mother listening to them. Rebecca was going to finish with Fraser when she went to university. It was a curiously empty relationship, not based on passion, something Rebecca was looking forward to experiencing one day.

Her mother had been listening to Classic FM – a Mahler symphony, Rebecca didn't know which one. She didn't like Mahler. Rebecca whisked the hot chocolate into a pan of milk. Her mother had a still-warm cup of camomile tea next to her pile of marking. *'Update* Romeo and Juliet *to the modern-day world'*. Oh for Christ's sake, they'd just write about the Baz Luhrmann film. Or Northern Ireland, or Bosnia, except they wouldn't know where that was. How clichéd. Why couldn't they just study the bloody text? *You have to make literature relevant to real life.* Why? Rebecca leafed idly through the top essay, a scrawled, messy affair. She smirked at the conclusion, 'What a sheer, big waste of love Romeo and Juliet is!' What a moron.

She could hear her mother's one-sided conversation with Simon, her mother on her side of the door remonstrating with that reasonable whine in her voice, Simon on the other side grunting like pre-literate Cro-Magnon man. In fact, if you thought of Simon as an unsuccessful example of Early Man his entire existence was easier to make sense of.

Her mother plodded back down the stairs. Rebecca could only see her legs through the banisters – white and veined, and her ankles like melting Brie above those bloody awful faux-Birkenstocks. She sighed as she came into the kitchen. Her mother had a huge lexicon of sighs. A sigh for every occasion. Her Simon sigh was always a particularly heavy one.

He's got Standard Grades next year, she said, as if Rebecca might be interested, as if Rebecca was the other parent for God's sake.

'Like I care.'

You didn't think to ask if I wanted any hot chocolate then? her mother said, adding a *no one in this house ever thinks about me* sigh.

'You've got camomile tea.' *The only conversations we ever have are arguments, have you ever thought about that, Rebecca?* 'Well, maybe that's your fault, have you ever thought about that, "Mother"?'

Rebecca left the kitchen abruptly. She wasn't going to give her mother the satisfaction of any kind of conversation. She slammed her bedroom door. 'Why don't you just die,' she muttered. 'Drop dead of a brain haemorrhage and leave us to get on with our lives.'

Simon turned his stereo up. Machine Head, *The Burning Red*. Boak's first album, *Guts for Garters*. He got into bed without bothering to undress and fell asleep imagining he was Eddie Gordo kicking and spinning and punching to his own beat. One day everyone would know the name of Simon McFarlane. Know it and fear it.

Slipknot, for God's sake. Surely their mother wasn't going to let him play that junk so loud at this time of night? What did the neighbours think? (God, had she really just thought that?) She put her headphones on and fell asleep listening to the 'Goldberg' Variations.

A nice family dinner. Nothing special.

But Beardy Brian wasn't family. He was a bloody stranger. A bloody stranger who was doing it with their mother – no, don't let your thoughts even go there, Simon.

Try and sit up straight, Simon. You'll give yourself back problems when you're older. 'I'm not going to be older.' *Don't be silly.*

Silly? That was her, with her manners and her rules and conscience. *Privileges come with duties attached.* What the fuck did that mean? Silly was what Beardy Brian made her. She had new clothes on – some kind of weird ethnic shite, and make-up which she only usually put on for parents' evenings – theirs and hers. And he knew for a fact that she had new underwear because he'd seen La Senza carrier bags all over the place. Don't go there, Simon.

Beardy Brian was so boring. He was some kind of social worker, so that suited his mother down to the ground. He was gulping the good red that she'd bought two bottles of from Oddbins, instead of her usual cheap stuff from Somerfield, for the *family dinner* and talking earnestly at her. 'They've ring-fenced the funding for youth work but that's not good enough you need a much bigger investment blah blah blah.' She loved all that stuff. *Oh, it's not even a case of investment – although it is, of course – it's more to do with imagination, these kids have been abandoned by society and then people condemn them for asocial behaviour –*

'I know, I know, it's ridiculous, Pam.' And on and on. Big yawn. Pam and Brian. The perfect couple.

'For God's sake, Simon,' his sister snarled, 'close your mouth when you eat. I really don't need to see the contents of your stomach.'

His sister actually believed she was a grown-up. Rebecca was going to be just like their mother when she did grow up. Ha ha. That would be funny – the worst thing she could ever think of was going to happen to her. That would serve her right. *They used to be so close when they were little.* Yeah, right, I don't think so. *Couldn't you just once make an effort?* At least Beardy Brian for dinner meant that they were having a roast. Roast Pork. Sweet. They hadn't had that since their father left. Funny that. Rebecca had some piece of vegetarian crap in a foil container.

'You'll fart all night,' he snickered at her.

Simon! 'What? It's a natural bodily function. We all fart. You fart all the time.' *Simon!*

Beardy Brian looked embarrassed. 'She does,' Simon said. 'You'll find out. If you haven't already.'

Simon. Enough!

Awkward silence, awkward for them anyway. Simon didn't feel awkward, he just wanted to get as much dead pig down his throat as fast as possible. 'Fatal wind.' Simon giggled. *I'm sorry?* 'Tekken,' Simon said. 'It's a character you can get called Panda. Panda's cool, he can crush you to death. Plus he farts. Fatal wind.' *He's a good boy really. He's just at that age.* She'd made pudding too. Tiramisu. Could almost be the name of a Tekken fighter. He heh, heh, heh. 'Won't you share the joke, Simon?' Beardy Brian, being all chummy. *Boys have it very difficult these days, Brian.* 'Tell me about it, Pam. Sometimes you wonder if they didn't have it right in the old days, channel all that testosterone, Spartan youth, Achilles, Herakles . . . warriors.' Warriors, my arse, what did Beardy Brian know about warriors? Simon was a warrior, oh yes. *Oh, I don't know about that, Brian, there's never anything good about fighting.* 'No such thing as a just war, Pam?' *Yes, but violence is a* final *resort, Brian, surely?*

He was divorced but he didn't have any kids. *You haven't missed anything, Brian.* Did they really do it together? Beardy Brian with his beer belly – oh, sorry, 'real ale' belly – it couldn't be the same as sex between attractive people, it must be a completely different activity. Shagging his mother— Stop! Don't go there!

No, but, really, it couldn't be like shagging Buffy, not that Simon wanted to shag Buffy (putting aside the fact she'd beat the crap out of him), she was too – what? Noble. Special. And heroic and vulnerable. You'd shag Romney Wright, you'd shag the women in porn mags, you wouldn't shag Buffy, you'd *court* her. Simon felt very pleased with that word. Court.

Simon, you've got gravy all down your chin.

Rebecca yelped with laughter. What a wanker. Simon had several astonishing new spots that had erupted on his forehead like plague pustules. He was like some kind of bio-hazard. Pus at one end, methane at the other. *Exclusion's all very well, but how do you get them back into education?* Jesus, was it possible to have a more boring conversation? They were having sex, she knew that, it was an appalling thought but there was no doubt about it. She had heard them – eugh – they were trying to be quiet but her mother's bed was right next to the wall on the other side of Rebecca's so she couldn't help but hear the snuffling and shuffling and shushing, her mother's suppressed giggles, *Oh, God, don't look – keep the light off!* And the occasional tenor cry from him that sounded like pain. How could they sully her sleep like that? Even with the headphones on, even with Haydn's Second Cello Concerto, Coldplay, Spiritualized, Mozart's Flute Concerto in A – dear God, she'd tried everything – nothing muffled the fact that her mother was having it off with Beardy Brian less than a metre away from her head. How gross was that? Not even Slipknot could have exorcised that fact.

And had she thought of the consequences? Like, was she through the menopause? She looked like she was but maybe she wasn't. What if their mother got pregnant? Could Rebecca think of anything worse? Apart from failing her Highers, which was obviously not going to happen.

But perhaps Beardy Brian was better than Hawk. Hawk (like he'd been christened that, yeah, right), that lunatic aberration of last year after their father left. Hawk, the guy she had hired to do all those little odd jobs that somehow in her mind had been the responsibility of their father, which was a ridiculous flaw in her memory as their father, an advocate in the High Court, had never lifted a screw-driver in his life.

Hawk was one of those loser hippy guys, all smug, cool, Zen philosophy and lazy smiles. You could tell he thought he was feline and irresistible but he must have been, God, at least thirty-five. He was the kind of guy who did it any-where with anyone. Even their mother. He'd even tried it on with Rebecca one time when he was fixing a leaking tap in the bathroom, which, by the way, had leaked twice as much after he'd finished with it. He hadn't touched her or any-thing, he'd just said, Do you want to?, just like that. As if.

She'd heard them in *the reading group*, talking about him, her mother laughing, *it must be because he's got a toolbox*, and them all creasing themselves as if it was some kind of fantastic joke and one of them saying, 'Go, girlfriend,' like they were *black* or something when they were all just Corstorphine teacher-types. Once a month *a pot-luck supper* on a *revolving rota* at each other's houses. All they did was eat and drink (like fish) and gossip and poke into each other's bathrooms and wardrobes and lifestyles. They gave the book about ten minutes – *Captain Corelli*, *The God of Small Things*, *White Teeth* – nothing that wasn't popular and safe and digested by someone else first. Like Beardy Brian.

Aren't you going to have some tiramisu, Becca?

'It's delicious,' Beardy Brian said, wiping his beard with a napkin. Oh, God, no, they had photographs out now.

Photographs of themselves as students – Beardy Brian, bearded and boring even then, her mother all long hair and indifferent features. *Oh, God, look at that cloak I'm wearing! A cloak, for heaven's sake!* Her mother's forearm touching Brian's shirtsleeve. What had Dad ever *seen* in her?

'You were always the brainy one, Pam.'

Why, thank you, kind sir. Yuck. Still, perhaps Beardy Brian would cushion their mother from Dad's news. If anyone ever got round to telling her. Jenny was five months gone already. Jenny, attractive and smart and fifteen whole years younger than their mother. Rebecca quite liked Jenny.

Where are you going, Simon? 'Out.' *We haven't finished.* 'I have.' *I thought we agreed you were grounded.* 'You agreed.' *What are you going to be doing, Simon? Are you meeting Jake and Angus? Simon, can you hear me?* 'Oh, shut the fuck up, will you.'

'Simon!' Beardy Brian rose half out of his chair to remonstrate.

'Don't you tell me what to do, you're not my dad.' *No and I don't see your father in this room, do you, Simon?* 'No, he's with his bloody girlfriend, probably looking at bloody Mothercare shite.'

Rebecca would have hit him if he'd been close enough. She could see that he was near to tears, he couldn't stop his lip trembling and his spots looked as if they were going to explode.

What are you talking about? Where are you going? Come back, Simon. Simon!

The clatter and rumble of Simon's skateboard faded down the street. 'Jenny's pregnant,' Rebecca said in a flat voice, avoiding eye contact, looking at the pepper grinder instead. She could feel her mother deflate. Beardy Brian was looking ill at ease. Rebecca couldn't imagine he would actually want to be part of this *family*.

Rebecca cleared away the dishes from the table. She hated the way her mother looked so pathetically grateful for this act.

You were very lucky. An unofficial warning and no record. We don't have to tell the school. 'First offence – what are they gonna do, bang me up for life?' *They probably only let you get away with it because your father was there. What's the point of being an advocate if you can't help your own child?* 'Yeah, good old Dad. Shame you had to cry all over him. "Oh, Alistair, Alistair." Pathetic.' *Promise me you will never, ever—* 'Yeah, yeah, yeah, never do it again, cross my heart and hope to die blah blah blah. One fucking CD.'

'How can she *believe* it was one CD?'

'Fuck off, Rebecca.'

'Fuck off yourself, Simon. You've stolen God knows how much stuff, your room's full of it – CDs, games, clothes – she thinks Dad's paying for it, it's not like he doesn't give you money, but I mean she must be stupid or really naive – which she is, we know—'

'Rebecca?'

'What?'

'Shut the fuck up, will you.'

'No, I won't, it's time somebody said something to you.'

'Oh and you're that person, are you? I don't think so. You think you're so bloody perfect. You and your friends. You swagger around school like you're so special.' Hannah, Sarah, Emma. God, how Simon hated them, always sniggering at him, laughing at everything he said, treating him like an idiot. 'A fine example of Early Man. Ha ha.'

'What have my friends got to do with anything?'

Hannah-Sarah-Emma – one entity in Simon's head. They were all going to be so sorry one day. He was going to punch them and kick them like Paul Phoenix kicking Ling Xiaoyu until they shut their mouths. That would surprise them. Or shag the lot of them – and they'd all think he was fantastic – Hannah-Sarah-Emma, all tossing their shiny hair and going down on him and moaning, a lot of moaning—

'Well? Can't you speak?'

'Shut up.'

'You're so articulate, Simon.'

'You're such a bitch.'

'You're such a wanker.'

'Cow.'

'Prick.'

'Whore.'

'Virgin.'

'Cunt.'

Simon? Simon? Did you just call your sister what I think you called her?

'Cunt, Mother,' Rebecca said sweetly, passing her mother on the stairs, 'he called me a cunt.'

Deftones. Tekken. A Pot Noodle. Another Pot Noodle. Half a sliced pan loaf with butter and jam. One illicit can of lager. Three illicit fags smoked out of the window. One last round of Tekken. Sleep. Dreams of world dominance and Hannah-Sarah-Emma giving him a blow job.

Mozart's *Requiem*. *Portrait of a Lady*. An apple. Half a bar of Dairy Milk. The cat purring on the bed. Hot chocolate and a small neatly rolled joint. Sleep. Dreams of the Chinese boy who sometimes delivered their takeaway and saving Simon from the Forth in flood. He was so dream-heavy that she thought she might have to let him slip back into the water. Then she woke up.

Rebecca ate a peach for breakfast. 'No Brian?' *No*. Her mother was sitting at the table reading the *Guardian* and eating muesli that looked like chicken feed. 'But it's Saturday morning.' *So?* Rebecca shrugged. Beardy Brian always stayed on a Friday night but she didn't really care enough to enter into a conversation about his absence. *It's a lovely day.* 'Mm.' Rebecca gave the cat a saucer of milk. *We could go to something in the Festival this morning.* 'I'm going to something already.' Her mother looked at her over the top of her glasses, smiling, very teacher. *Oh, what?* All excited and interested. 'Mozart Quartets. Queen's Hall.' *Well, maybe I could come with you?* 'Sold out.' *Oh. Are you going with Fraser?* 'Fraser? No.'

Simon at the bus stop, head full of nothing, arms full of skateboard. There was a couple ahead of him in the queue who were trying to see how far down each other's throats they could get. Disgusting. The old people waiting for the 41 shuffled discontentedly at this display of tonsil hockey. Simon liked that phrase, tonsil hockey. It was stupid and it removed any potential for tenderness. They were two of the ugliest people he'd ever seen. They were both dressed in black. The guy was tall and hairy and young with an Iron Maiden T-shirt. The girl was huge. Fat. Simon just wanted to stare at her arse and thighs. What a bloater! And not bonny, oh no. It must be like shagging a bouncy castle. And her norks! Like a hundred times bigger than his sister's. Why was he thinking about his sister's norks? Gross. He could see the tonsil hockey girl's nipples through her black top. Smuggling bullets. Heh, heh, heh.

'Your type, is she?'

Fucking Rebecca. 'Fuck off.' The old people shuffled more agitatedly, one or two of them muttered about Simon's language, about Rebecca's queue jumping. The 41 sailed into view and Simon made a point of not letting the old people on first, mumbling 'Day Saver' at the bus driver and rushing up the stairs to get away from his sister.

'Don't mind me sitting here, do you?' Rebecca said. Full of herself. She got off four stops ahead of him. Neither of them enquired where the other was going.

Simon got off on the George IV bridge and walked down the Royal Mile where he met Jake and Angus in the Games Workshop. In the international newsagents Simon lifted three Cadbury's Twirls, a Bounty, a packet of salted peanuts and a can of Irn-Bru, and a *Paris Match* just for the hell of it. After a lot of mindless, spaceless time they moved on and got thrown out of Starbucks. In Bristo Square they finally got round to skateboarding. Simon didn't have pads or a helmet, no way was he going to wear that stuff where people could see him.

Queen's Hall Festival-goers – what were they like, milling around on the pavement outside the concert venue like a flock of sheep, waiting to be let in. They were all so early, it wasn't like the tickets didn't have seat numbers on, for God's sake. No way was she going to hang around like that. She went for a coffee in a nearby café. A guy came in and sat at the table opposite. Rebecca would lay a bet that he was going to the concert too. She wished it wasn't people like her mother and Beardy Brian who liked classical music. This guy was bearded too. He was drinking a milky coffee and eating some kind of Danish pastry. Apricot. Little flakes of pastry fell into his beard. Gross. The guy was overweight, he shouldn't be eating stuff like that.

KO. You Lose. Game Over. Simon flew through the air and heard rather than felt his face slamming into the pavement. A second before that came the 'oh, shit' moment, when you knew it was too late and there was nothing you could do about it. Then the moment when you cast your mind back to the previous second to try to work out what went wrong. Uneven pavement probably. Edinburgh's pavements were crap. Could he have— but no because that moment was past and he was in the pure empty space of shock. He knew he should enjoy it because it wasn't going to la— too painful to scream so the scream was all inside his head. Jesus, Jesus, Jesus. Jake and Angus bending over him. Jake laughing. 'Good one, bonehead.' Angus not laughing. Angus looking like he was going to boak. 'Jesus, Simon, what a fucking mess.' Passers-by, better equipped with brains, coming to his rescue, thank fuck. Someone wanting him to walk to the A and E, 'It's just a couple of hundred yards, son,' a woman getting all bossy talking about neck collars and fractured skulls. Warm metallic blood in his mouth and all his head rearranged. A doctor appeared, out of breath, he must have run from the hospital.

Simon's phone was in his hand, he had no idea how it got there, the screen was cracked. He gave it to a white-faced Angus. He was gargling blood and there were teeth in his mouth that weren't attached to anything. He held up a finger to Angus and Angus actually understood. 'Speed dial one?' Simon grunted. Speed dial 1. 'MUM' it said on the screen.

The Queen's Hall was packed, the air hot and expectant. That moment of quiet when people gather themselves together and wait. You could power generators on that energy. The Queen's Hall was some kind of church once and you could feel something now, like prayer, willing transformation to occur. Rebecca was standing in the gallery, the cheapest tickets. In the seated parts of the gallery she could see her English teacher, Mr Petrie, from school, looking like he was going to boak (rumour had it that he was dying), Hannah's father with a woman she'd never seen before (file that one away for later), a Gothy couple who looked completely out of place but whom she recognized from somewhere – dressed all in black, him with an Iron Maiden T-shirt, her incredibly fat (how did you get that fat? just by eating?) – and yes indeed, the bearded man from the café, standing on the opposite side of the gallery. Down in the body of the kirk (as you didn't often get to say in a non-metaphorical way), she could see her first music teacher, who she thought was dead, and the boy of her dreams, the Chinese guy who delivered their takeaway (now that *was* interesting).

The four musicians walked on and the quiet changed to stern, energetic applause. Two women, two men, foreign, all funereal, their thoughts in some other, internal universe (perhaps she should have applied to music college, after all). One woman beautiful, one so-so, both men ugly-ish. No beards. They settled onto their uncomfortable-looking chairs, they adjusted their instruments, they raised their bows – another moment of stillness, absolute this time so that nothing of those first hushed notes of the Adagio would be lost, the cello pulsating on the air, the dissonances building from the violins and the viola – crescendo, drop a step, cello repeating, building, rising, melancholic – Rebecca felt as if she might be about to have a vision, her whole body had lifted a few inches into the air. Only when the sweetness of the Allegro took over, drenching everyone and everything in sunshine, could she relax, safe in the knowledge she wasn't going to float away. The world could not end as long as the 'Dissonant Quartet' was being played.

'Dislocated jaw, broken nose, fractured left cheekbone, hairline fracture to the skull, front teeth gone, bit of your tongue gone – nasty one, that – try to put your hands out to save yourself next time, better still wear the right gear. We'll have to keep you in, obviously, keep an eye on the skull fracture, you don't feel sick at all? Seeing double? Good. Any questions?'

'More morphine?' Except what came out of his mouth didn't sound like language.

'Ha, ha. I'll leave you with Mum now.' The blur of white coat disappeared. *Don't try to talk, darling.* Cool hand stroking his forehead, hot tears rolling down the sides of his face, pooling in his ears. *Everything's all right. Don't talk.* He held his mother's hand. *Hush.*

And then the Allegro molto. And it was all about closing now and trying to make the most of it because it would finish and really you just wanted it to go on for ever – the bearded man from the café was staring goggle-eyed at her. She closed her eyes. Idiot. But . . . she opened her eyes. He was clutching his chest, rigid with terror. He looked as if he might be about to fall headlong over the rail but he staggered into the person next to him, who glared silently in that middle-class way. Rebecca moved fast, round the back of the gallery. By the time she reached him someone had helped him out but he had only got as far as the top of the stairs outside the exit, where he sat now like a man who wasn't accustomed to sitting on stairs. He looked peculiarly unloved. And then he slumped, to a little gasp from the people trying to minister to him. An usher said she'd phoned for an ambulance, someone felt ineffectually for a pulse. The man was the colour of newly poured concrete.

Someone was obviously going to have to do something.

'Undo his collar and tie, loosen his belt,' Rebecca said. People looked at her warily. 'It's OK, I'm a trained first-aider,' she snapped. Which was true. She felt with two fingers for the pulse in his neck. Nothing. She checked his chest for breath-signs. Nothing. She tilted his head back and exhaled into his mouth. She could taste coffee and sugar, she could taste the apricot pastry. Gross. She compressed his chest, one-two-three-four-five, one breath, one-two-three-four-five compressions, one breath. She squeezed his heart and gave him her breath and kept on doing so because he wasn't coming back to life like he was supposed to.

The Coda opened – the man was dying to the accompaniment of Mozart – sublime cadence fell on sublime cadence. If she had to die, Rebecca hoped it would be to Mozart. The final cadence, the quick clean ending and then the applause flooding the out-of-sight auditorium. You wouldn't want to die to the sound of applause. A paramedic ran up the stairs towards her. 'Heart attack,' she said, matter-of-factly, between breaths, between compressions. He spoke television dialogue to her, 'I'll take over from here,' and she stood up, suddenly dizzy.

More television dialogue – 'I've got a pulse,' the paramedic said, glancing up at Rebecca, 'well done.' People murmured praise, someone asked her if she was OK, but she was already gone, stumbling down the stairs, her own healthy heart thudding, out of the door into fine rain and a weak, watery sun and the traffic jammed on Clerk Street. She could hardly breathe, as if the bearded man had taken all of her breath and left her none. She thought she was giving him the gift of life but now it felt as if it was the other way round. And anyway she wasn't sure she wanted the gift of life. Or the gift of death. She didn't want that kind of power, she didn't want to be like a god. What the fuck would she do with that kind of responsibility? She walked quickly, the tears rolling down her face, unchecked.

V

SHEER BIG WASTE OF LOVE

Nunc scio quid sit amor

VIRGIL

DDISON FOX WAS NAMED FOR HIS FATHER. BILL Addison refused to have anything to do with his unlooked-for son but Addison's mother, Shirley, was determined to get Addison's father's name on his birth certificate, one way or another. Addison met his father only once, when he was seven years old – an encounter so traumatic (Addison, his mother and a relatively innocent bystander ended up in the casualty department of the local hospital) that Addison lost any further desire to be acquainted with his reluctant father.

Paternity, in general, wasn't a subject that Addison had ever given much thought to until he found that he was going to be a father himself. When he celebrated his fortieth birthday Addison had neither child nor wife. When he celebrated his forty-first he had both, one inside the other. Every morning when Addison woke up he was surprised anew by these two facts.

Addison had been courted, bedded and wedded in haste by a primary-school teacher called Clare Soutar. Addison met her when he gave her a speeding ticket on the M8. Addison never did understand how she had got his phone number out of him (it was against so many rules it didn't bear thinking about) but he seemed to remember that it was some ruse about coming to her school to give a talk to the children about what it was like to be a traffic policeman.

Clare, Addison very soon discovered, ran her entire life at breakneck speed. By the time they were sprinting up the aisle he had begun to wonder if she didn't have some kind of metabolic disease. 'Well, neither of us are getting any younger, Addison,' she said, when she proposed to him after two months of hectic dating.

Addison spent several evenings of their early courtship helping with lesson preparation. At the time, Clare had been doing a project on the Ancient Greeks with her Primary Sevens – cutting and pasting pictorial maps of a Greek city state, constructing a Trojan horse out of ice-lolly sticks, making chitons out of sheets and temples out of the cardboard tubes from kitchen rolls, and mounting dramatic little playlets about the adventures of the gods. Addison learnt a lot from this project – geometry, epic poetry, metempsychosis, to name but three things – and wondered how he had lived all his life in Edinburgh without knowing anything about Greek columns. 'Doric, Ionic, Corinthian,' he explained to his partner, Robbie, one afternoon as they crawled up the Mound, escorting a car containing some minor royal, 'take the National Gallery for example, the volutes on that are—' until Robbie told him that he really didn't give a shite what the vol-au-vents on the National Gallery were. Addison reckoned that if he stuck with Clare he might make up for the education he had mysteriously bypassed at an earlier age. If he was lucky, he thought, he might make up for some of the mothering he lacked as well.

Clare herself was from a family that was top-heavy with competent maternal women. Her mother was a district nurse, one sister, Fiona, was an assistant bank manager, another, Kirsty, a social worker. Clare's father was a meek, bemused man who submitted willingly to female authority. 'Best just to give in to them,' he confided to Addison, over his first family dinner, 'makes for a much easier life.'

'Clare's always liked a man in uniform,' her mother said to Addison.

'Oh yeah,' Fiona laughed casually, 'she's had a fireman, that guy that was in the navy, even that history lecturer was in the TA, wasn't he?'

'A sergeant in the traffic division's a good one, though,' Kirsty said, as if Addison was part of a set to be collected. Addison stared at his plate of pork casserole and mashed potatoes and felt slightly sick.

'He's sitting right in front of you,' Clare rebuked mildly and she caught Addison's eye and winked at him. It struck him that he knew absolutely nothing about family life. He supposed this was something else he was going to have to learn.

It was only when Clare was drawing up the seating plan for the church that Addison's truly remarkable absence of relatives became apparent to her. They had been so busy getting to know each other in the details (a shared hatred of mushrooms, a love of fairground rides and so on) that the bigger things (Addison's orphan status, Clare's diabetes) had got slightly overlooked.

'No one at all?' she frowned. Addison shook his head.

'Not even a second cousin three times removed?'

No one, he assured her. Which was a lie, but it was so much easier than the truth. Addison simplified his life story for Clare – he had been illegitimate (a fact borne out by his birth certificate), his mother died the week before his eighth birthday, when no one came forward to claim him he had been sent to a vicious Catholic orphanage where he had stayed until his sixteenth birthday. At the age of twenty he decided he had a choice between following a life of crime or becoming a policeman, and had chosen the latter. He was a beat sergeant before transferring to traffic where he had served six out of the seven years he was allowed. When he left traffic he was hoping to become a dog handler. He liked dogs, he didn't like traffic. After six years he thought it was normal to die in a car crash. Addison didn't think it was healthy to think like that.

'And your mother,' Clare said, puzzled, 'she never said who your father was?'

'Never,' Addison said.

Shirley talked about Addison's father a lot. 'Your father' she would say to Addison, in a way that sounded oddly formal. Bill Addison had been a fighter pilot who after the war had turned his mechanic's hand to cars, starting with a modest garage on the A1 on the way out of Edinburgh and building to a small empire dotted all around the city. For a brief period – in his self-penned advertising material – he was known as the Car King.

Occasionally, Bill Addison's photograph would appear in the paper – a Rotary Club dinner or the opening of a new garage – and Shirley would cut it out and keep it on the kitchen table – where most things were kept – and would brood over it for days before eventually tearing it up in a fit of bitterness and burning it on the fire. In the absence of any real facts from Shirley, Addison developed his own version of his father. A handsome war hero – Addison knew the type from comics – still fighting a war somewhere (despite the Rotary Club dinners) and thus unable to return to his loving wife and son. Addison imagined him high in the clouds, like a god in his chariot, overseeing all his son did. One day he would drive up their street in a golden car (possibly with a crown on his head) and whisk them away to a much better life.

Addison eavesdropped for additional information, for

whenever Shirley's friend Mary came round in the evening to help Shirley work her way down to the bottom of a bottle of gin, the conversation would inevitably turn to Addison's paternity. 'Ha,' he heard his mother say once, 'he came in a fucking shower of gold,' and Mary said, 'I hope you made him pay extra,' and they both howled with laughter and choked on their cigarettes and gin. Another time, Mary (who seemed to know his father almost as well as Shirley did) complained that Bill Addison didn't think he was subject to the same rules as 'mere mortals'.

'Aye,' Shirley agreed, 'his sort always gets away with it.'

The wedding was like a school project on a large scale and Clare and her family approached it with an efficiency and economy that would have been sorely coveted by Addison's chief inspector. Addison was dragged round the stalls of one wedding fair after another by Clare and forced to help her choose 'favour baskets' and 'colour-coordinated balloons' and God knows what other stuff he had never suspected existed. She cut articles from bridal magazines with titles like 'Ways To Panic Proof Your Wedding' and 'Ten Things To Consider Before You Say I Do' and Addison had begun to think that the strategic-planning stage would go on for ever when suddenly he found himself standing at the altar wondering if she would see sense and jilt him at the last minute.

It was a church wedding even though Clare was a professed atheist, something she refrained from telling the Church of Scotland minister. There was a fast and furious ceilidh at the reception and Addison was introduced to more Soutars than he thought it was possible for one country to contain.

Before he knew it, the wedding was over and they were on a plane bound for some Greek island the name of which Addison had missed. When Addison woke up on the first morning of his honeymoon he felt completely disorientated, as if he had been on a long journey through space and time and had been dropped back down to earth into another life altogether. A life where an unknown woman was snoring gently next to him in a bed that was on fire with foreign sunlight.

His own mother had never had a honeymoon or a wedding, never been a bride or a wife. Shirley had been a prostitute. He didn't tell Clare this, not because he was ashamed, Addison knew no woman walked the streets from anything less than dire necessity, but because he thought it was no one's business other than Shirley's. What puzzled Addison, given the nature of his mother's profession, was why his mother had been so grimly certain about the source of his paternity.

Only with hindsight did Addison understand the reason for his one and only visit to his father. His mother must have known she was dying and she had been trying to find another home for her only child. When he thought about this it made him feel unbearably sad, not for himself, but for his mother.

Addison and his mother caught a bus and travelled to the other side of Edinburgh, where the broad, tree-lined streets and the big houses with their abundant summer gardens seemed to Addison to belong to a quite different city from the one where he lived, in a dark tenement in which you could smell the docks but not see the water.

His mother had started off the journey in good spirits but was soon in the grip of a fretful anxiety. Shirley's moods were as changeable as the capital's weather and she could move from wild elation to spiteful malevolence in the time it took Addison to scurry out into the security of the street where he would loiter until it seemed safe to go home. By the age of five Addison was adept at loitering.

After what seemed an eternity to Addison, they finally alighted from the bus. He was disappointed to discover that they hadn't arrived at their destination and still had an endless walk down several more of those broad, tree-lined streets. Addison wondered who it was that lived amongst this opulence of blossom trees and how his mother could possibly know them.

It was a Sunday and the air was full of noises that were foreign to Addison's ears – the soothing rhythm of push-

and-pull lawnmowers and the clarion call of church bells. The scents of a Sunday in the suburbs were equally exotic – new-mown grass, lilacs and the tantalizing aroma of roasting meat. Addison was very hungry. Addison was always hungry. Shirley's idea of breakfast was a slice hacked off a white loaf, scraped with margarine and sprinkled with sugar. Sometimes she didn't even remember that, and Addison had to make do with the small bottle of playground milk at school break-time. If Shirley forgot to feed him at the weekend or in the school holidays then Addison could go hungry all day, although, often as not, one of the women in the street where he lived would throw him down a jeelie piece or a sixpence for a poke of chips. Addison was called 'the poor wee wean' more often than he was ever called Addison.

This morning a restless, festive mood had led Shirley to buy lardy Aberdeen rolls from the corner shop but she had rushed Addison to the bus stop before he'd had time to tear off more than one mouthful.

Addison began to lag behind. The steel tips of his mother's stiletto heels made a brutish noise on the street. All Shirley's shoes were the same – sharply pointed at the toe and with heels that were precariously, ludicrously high. She was forever staggering and turning her ankle or tripping on cracks in the pavement and if she wanted to run for the bus she had to take her shoes off and sprint in her stockinged feet. When she died, a year later, Addison could remember his mother's shoes long after he'd forgotten her face.

Shirley yanked him by the hand, 'Come *on*, Addison,' she said, and Addison heard the tetchy note in her voice that meant it would be best for him to trot along as fast as possible.

Eventually, they came to a halt in front of a tall wrought-iron gate. Shirley lit a nervous cigarette and alternated between smoking it and chewing her lip while staring at the gate, lost in agitated thought. Addison had once heard a neighbour refer to his mother as 'highly strung' and although he had no idea what that meant he knew it sounded like an uncomfortable thing to be.

As if she'd come to a decision, Shirley threw the half-smoked cigarette down and ground it into the pavement with the sole of one pointed shoe. She checked her make-up and her hair in her compact mirror and straightened the little jacket she was wearing over her smartest dress – a striped shirtwaister with three-quarter sleeves and a stiff collar that had been fashionable several years before Addison's birth. Addison always thought of his mother as a young woman and was surprised when many years later he realized that she was forty when she died, only a year younger than Addison was now. She was a drinker, of course, and, although the drink didn't kill her, it didn't help to stop the cancer already racing round her body on that summer Sunday morning.

She snapped the compact shut. 'Right,' she said, to herself rather than Addison. She swung open the wrought-iron gate and walked briskly up the path, her heels striking like flints off the slabs of York stone, but her purposefulness seemed to evaporate when she reached the front door, where she stopped, looking suddenly forlorn, like someone who had been locked out rather than someone who was trying to get in. 'Christ, Addison,' she muttered to him as if he were a fellow adult, 'I could do with a fucking drink.'

The door was a massy, ornate affair in heavily varnished wood and it reminded Addison of the bank in town that his mother took him to sometimes. Shirley, as with many other things in her life, went into the bank with high hopes and invariably came out with them dashed. She would enquire of one of the blank-faced cashiers in a tight, strained voice – a sorry attempt at refinement – as to whether any money had 'come into her account' and when the answer was no (Addison had never known it to be yes), she would storm out, ranting and cursing in language that passers-by seemed to find shocking beyond belief, although it sounded fairly run-of-the-mill to Addison's ears.

Shirley tilted her head to one side as if listening out for something. Unconsciously, Addison imitated her pose. He heard people close by, people who seemed to be enjoying themselves – the booming, bass laughter of a man, the pleasant, melodious voices of women, quite different from Shirley's gravelly smoker's timbre. And, further off, the high notes of children playing, a noise that made Addison perk up like an eager dog.

They followed the thread of voices along a narrow stone-chip path that took them round the corner of the pink sandstone wall of the house. The house had a small tower and what looked like battlements and Addison wondered if it was a castle. Shirley hesitated in front of yet another door – a planked wooden one set into a wall. The house might as well have had moat, drawbridge and portcullis for all the difficulties it seemed intent on throwing in her path.

The voices that had lured them were coming from the other side of the wall. Addison heard the clinking of glasses and the ambrosial scent of food. His stomach groaned. 'Sh,' his mother whispered, as if his hunger was something under his control. She gave Addison a critical look and then searched for a handkerchief in her handbag, spat on it, and rubbed Addison's face. She flattened his unruly hair with the palm of her hand, knocking him off balance as she did so. Shirley frowned, unable to see much improvement. She bent down to speak in Addison's ear, an action that made him take an involuntary step backwards.

'Remember,' she cautioned, as if they had discussed the subject beforehand (which Addison was sure they hadn't), 'stand up straight and look him in the eye when he speaks to you. OK?'

'OK,' Addison agreed.

From beyond the wall, there was a sudden burst of laughter as if the punchline of a joke had just been delivered. Shirley took a fortifying breath. 'Right then,' she said, 'time to confront his majesty in all his glory,' and she pushed open the wooden door.

There seemed to be a consensus amongst the nuns in the orphanage that Addison's mother was in hell, an idea so horrifying that Addison tried never to think about it. Now, now that the nuns' brainwashing had (more or less) left his system, he knew Shirley was neither in hell, nor heaven – she was nowhere, she was dead. In some ways he preferred the idea that she was in hell because then at least she would exist.

It was only after Clare's belly began to swell in the months following the wedding ('I'm too old to hang about, Addison') that Addison's own childhood – what little there was of it – began to occupy his mind. If his father had accepted his responsibilities that day, if he had welcomed Addison into his home, how different Addison's life would have been. He would have inhabited a world of golf and dinner-dances and good Edinburgh schools. He would have had brothers and sisters and a sense of belonging to something instead of always feeling like an outsider, an observer of other people's lives. He had thought that having Clare – and now this unknown, unimaginable baby – would change all that. But it didn't. Addison was still on the outside looking in.

Addison followed his mother and found himself standing on a lawn. Unless you counted the grass on Leith Links, Addison didn't think he'd ever stood on lawn before and his instinct was to kneel down and touch it. Instead, he pressed himself into Shirley's skirts and inhaled her smoky fragrance and silently took in the prospect before them, which, to Addison, looked like a picture from one of his mother's magazines – well-dressed people smoking and drinking and throwing their heads back in easy laughter. The women were sipping delicately from little glasses ('Sherry,' his mother said dismissively under her breath) while the men drank from big cut-glass tumblers.

'Ah, the old amber nectar, Bill,' one of the men said and they touched glasses, making a ringing sound like crystalline bells. Addison regarded 'Bill' with interest. He was a big man, bigger than the others, with the kind of imposing stature that intimidated other men. On the other hand, he didn't seem awfully heroic to Addison – the skin on his cheeks was pouchy and slack and his thinning hair was plastered to his scalp. In contrast, his face sported a huge beard.

There were children racing around the garden, playing a high-spirited game of catch. A boy held a toy aeroplane aloft as he ran and Addison watched its metal wings flashing in the sunshine and wondered if he would be allowed to join in.

For all the notice anyone was taking of Addison and his mother they might as well have been cloaked by an invisibility spell. Only one person seemed to see them – a small girl, two or three years old, who was sitting contentedly on a rug on the grass, playing with a doll. When she saw Addison she smiled and waved a clean, plump hand at him, almost as if she'd been expecting him. All the small children of Addison's acquaintance were grubby, snotty, bawling creatures who always smelt rank, but this girl was like a creature from another world. She was wearing a pristine pink dress that spread out around her on the rug like petals and looked as if she smelt of cake and sweets and flowers and other good things that Addison dreamed of.

Addison wondered if she had come from Fairyland – a place Addison knew about because his Primary One teacher, Miss Cameron, had read a story about it to her class (although she had felt it necessary to add the caveat that Fairyland didn't actually exist and was in contravention of all Biblical teaching).

'Don't look so glaikit, Addison,' his mother hissed at him.

Afterwards, a long, long time afterwards, Addison came to see this scene for what it was. A family gathered for Sunday lunch, enjoying a pre-prandial drink in the sunshine. At the time, however, it was as if that wooden door had opened on a vision of an unearthly kingdom, peopled by heavenly creatures, and, more than anything he had ever known, Addison wanted to step into that divine world and be a part of it.

A woman appeared at the French windows of the house

and came out onto the patio. She was wearing an apron and was holding a wooden spoon in her hand as if she had been tasting something. She called out gaily to the assembled company, 'Lunch is ready, everyone,' but then the cloak of invisibility must have dropped from their shoulders because the woman spotted Addison and Shirley and her hostess smile froze on her lips and her conviviality was replaced by a glacial mask that seemed to Addison to chill the air around him. Still clutching the wooden spoon in one hand, but now brandishing it like a weapon, she called to the little girl ('Susan!') and when Susan didn't respond she hurried to scoop her up protectively, keeping her eyes fixed on Shirley, as if she was a dangerous wild animal that might pounce at any moment.

The woman called out sharply to her other children – 'Douglas! Andrew! Pamela!' – and three of the children who had been playing catch obediently detached themselves from the others and ran towards their mother. All three were older than Addison. The elder boy still had the toy aeroplane clutched in his hand and Susan, perched against her mother's chest, reached out to grab it. Addison suddenly felt the siren call of cells and DNA and blood and had to resist an almost overwhelming urge to walk across the lawn and shoulder his way into the middle of this little group and become part of Bill Addison's family.

'It's all right, Marjorie,' Bill Addison said, striding across the lawn like a man intent on defending his property. A great cloud passed suddenly over the face of the sun and Addison shivered.

If you ignored the increasingly absurd wooden spoon that Marjorie Addison was holding aloft, she struck an imperious maternal figure. Addison feared that Shirley would stand little chance of victory in any contest with her. There was such cruel fury in her eyes that it seemed to Addison that at any moment she might turn his mother into some helpless creature – a cow or a bear, or worse.

'Now look here,' Bill Addison said angrily to Shirley, 'I don't know what you want, but this is a private house.' There was a murmur of agreement from the assembled guests. The dark cloud grew darker. Addison felt a drop of rain splash on his cheek.

'You don't know what I want?' Shirley said, her voice cracking with disbelief. Addison saw a streak of lightning fracture the sky and almost immediately thunder banged so loudly that he felt his heart give an answering thump. Susan began to cry. Addison reached for his mother's hand for reassurance but she pulled herself away from him, advancing aggressively on a glowering Bill Addison. Addison followed his mother across the lawn.

'Stop right there, son.' Bill Addison loomed above him, so close that Addison smelt the alien male scent of pipe tobacco and Brylcreem and malt whisky. Addison was terrified, but he had heard that one word – *son*. This must be the moment (quite different from the one in his imagination) when his father was going to claim him as his own. Addison stood up straight and tried to look Bill Addison in the eye, an impossibility given the way his father was towering over him. Addison tried to think of the right thing to say but only one word came to his mind. 'Father,' he said, hearing how tinny and useless his voice sounded. Before he had a chance to compose anything else Bill Addison unleashed a blow like a thunderbolt (for a moment Addison wondered if he had actually been struck by lightning) and he found himself sprawled, full-length, on the lawn.

All Addison could see was a great bowl of purple, rain-darkened sky above his head. He could hear his mother spitting out obscenities. His father roared, 'Whore!' at her in an enraged, apoplectic tone and one of the women screamed in horror at the word, although not nearly as much as when his mother yelled back at his father that he was 'a fucking, cunting whoremaister'. The words sounded fuzzy to Addison, it was only later in the hospital that he discovered his eardrum had burst. Blood ran down his face from his nose and dripped onto the grass and when he tried to turn his head a spasm of hot pain shot through it. Tears started to roll down his face and mingle with the blood. The lawn, he noticed, was not as green close up as it had looked from a distance.

Then his mother screamed, 'Fucking rapist!' and Bill Addison began to hit Shirley. Addison heard someone say, 'Hang on there, Bill,' and get thumped for their trouble. A bolt of lightning rent a fissure across the sky. A thunderclap exploded above his head and Addison decided he was dead.

He was brought to life again by a deluge of rain. The smell of wet earth and grass was oddly comforting, although for the rest of his life a sudden summer downpour would make Addison's heart contract with an unnameable grief.

A pair of small feet appeared by his head. The feet were encased in frilled white socks and white Clark's sandals. Addison had never seen socks that white. The owner of the feet dropped to their knees by his side. Addison found himself looking up into Susan's solemn face. Her hair had been turned to wet strings by the rain and her pink dress now clung damply to her body. Silently, she placed the toy aeroplane on the grass next to him. Addison licked his dry lips and tried to form a word of thanks but then Susan was dragged away by her mother.

Addison had just arrived at an accident on the M9 when Clare went into premature labour. It was raining and they'd had a call on the radio to say 'the VA looks as if it's going to prove' (the 'fatal' was always left off the end of this sentence – Addison sometimes wondered if it was out of a kind of delicacy). By the time they had got there it was all over and there was nothing to do but stand around helplessly looking at the smashed-up Audi A4 and somebody's wife, somebody's mother lying all broken up on the road. Addison wished his own wife wouldn't drive so fast. That was when Robbie got the call to say that Clare had been taken into hospital and Addison thought there was something weird about that – the one life just ended, the other about to begin. What if the soul of this dead woman had flown into body of his own child? They didn't know if it was a boy or a girl because Clare wanted to be surprised. Addison wasn't so keen on surprises himself. He hoped it was a girl. Clare laughed and said she just hoped it was a baby.

It turned out that the one thing that Clare didn't do quickly was give birth. There were 'complications' but no one made it very clear what they were and Addison was left stranded in a small waiting room on his own. Addison was used to being in charge at accidents (this felt like an accident) and didn't know what to do with this powerlessness. He stared at the floor in front of his feet and found himself wondering if it was going to prove.

They nearly lost the baby, then they nearly lost Clare. Was that what she had been doing – racing against life, trying to keep one step ahead of the open grave? Eventually, Addison was taken to see her. She looked a strange green colour but she was all right. She smiled at him as if it was her role to cheer him up. Addison couldn't think of anything to say so he just sat by the bed holding her hand and must have fallen asleep because a nurse was shaking him gently awake and asking him if he'd like to see his son. For a minute Addison had no idea what she was talking about.

Despite the tubes and dials that adorned his ICU cot, the baby looked healthier than his mother. The nurse told Addison that he was going to pull through, in a way that seemed absurdly confident to Addison. Clare didn't seem so convinced either when he went back to her single-bedded room. Addison knew it wasn't a good sign that she was in a room on her own. He wondered if it would be better if he was more optimistic or would that be like asking for trouble?

Clare wanted to give the baby a name straight away but as neither of them wanted religion involved she suggested they put an announcement in the paper. Clare insisted that Addison decide on a name – they had already drawn up a shortlist of five – and Addison finally settled on Ewan because it seemed Scottish but not too Scottish. The outside world – wet and cold – hit Addison like a blow when he left the overheated bubble of the hospital. He really didn't know if he could take the lifetime of worry that lay ahead of him now that he had a child.

The next day Addison bought a copy of the *Evening News* to check the announcement was in. It was and it looked solid and certain. The baby existed, it had a name, a name in print. Addison had never in his life read the Births and Deaths column but now it took on a personal interest and he glanced idly through the list of names, vaguely curious about the children who shared a birth date with his own son – a Connor and an Amelia. His eye was caught by the first announcement in the Deaths column – 'Addison'. For a paranoid moment Addison thought it was some kind of foretelling of his own death and then he realized it was his father. His father was dead.

The funeral was in the crematorium. Addison sat in the back row, near the door. Marjorie Addison, now a bent and shrivelled figure, was seated at the front, nearest to the coffin. She had had to be supported into the crematorium by her two sons, Douglas and Andrew, one on either side of her, but now that she was seated it was her daughters who sat with her. Pam, frumpy in washed-out black, dabbed her eyes from time to time. Next to her Susan remained dry-eyed throughout, staring at the coffin with a kind of defiance.

Thanks to a short obituary piece in the *Evening News*, Addison knew that his father had handed on the garage empire to Douglas and Andrew ten years ago but right up to the end had interfered in the running of it ('never quite let go of the reins'). Addison's brothers sat with their heads bowed, unwaveringly solemn expressions fixed on their faces. Halfway through the service, Douglas glanced at his watch. They were both big, built like rugby players, but close up he could see they looked too paunchy to be really fit. Addison reckoned he could take both of them if he had to – not that he was planning to, but the last time he had made a claim to his birthright ('Father—') it had ended in violence and there was no guarantee it wouldn't go the same way this time.

The service was a perfunctory sort of affair, lacking in emotion and built out of clichés – 'pillar of the business community', 'stalwart of the Rotary Club', 'an Olympian'. Addison hoped that he wouldn't have a funeral service. Perhaps he could persuade Clare to take his body to some clifftop somewhere and build him a funeral pyre and set it alight in one last blaze of glory so that he could rise up into the atmosphere and circle the earth as dust and ashes. His father's body, on the other hand, encased in polyester satin and ash veneer, disappeared discreetly behind a blue velvet curtain to be incinerated out of sight.

As the mourners filed out, the minister took up a position by the door, like a good maître d', and Addison had to suppress an urge to tip him.

Addison followed the family back to the house. He found it hard to believe how much smaller it was than the baronial construct of his memory – no more than a detached Edinburgh villa with a few architectural curlicues.

As Addison started walking up the path his heart began to beat very fast and he found himself sweating inside his overcoat. He was gripped by an irrational fear that if he stepped over the threshold of his father's house he would be struck dead and it was only an act of sheer willpower that got him up the steps and through the glass doors of the porch.

The mourners were congregated in a large drawing room at the back of the house where a mock-Tudor bay looked out onto the garden, on which a winter gloom had already descended even though it was still early afternoon. The funeral tea was catered and the waiting staff moved quietly around the room, their expressions respectfully neutral. The atmosphere was that of a muted cocktail party.

Addison found himself standing near Pamela, Douglas and Andrew. Douglas and Andrew looked relieved, as if they couldn't wait to get on with their lives now.

'I never thought of him as someone who would die,' Pamela said.

'Well, it turns out that the old man was mortal like the rest of us,' Douglas said.

'You're so hard.'

'You should be harder.'

Douglas lit a cigarette and said, 'I thought he would never go.'

Andrew raised his glass to his brother in an ironic toast and murmured, 'The king is dead, long live the king.' Addison imagined the shock on their faces if he suddenly declared himself as one of them. But it was too late, and somehow it didn't mean anything any more. There was nothing left to do but leave.

Susan was standing at the open front door, holding a

bottle of malt. She was looking at the rain but when she saw Addison she smiled as if she'd been expecting him and offered him the malt. Addison shook his head, even though the whisky looked like the best thing he'd seen all day. Addison had been a teetotaller since attending his first fatal VA six years ago – three children from the back seat of a Nissan scattered all over the M90 thanks to a whisky-sodden accountant in a Mercedes. One of the children was still alive when Addison peeled her off the tarmac. Would Clare agree never to take their own child out in the car? Hardly likely.

He knew Susan had three children of her own. She was a lawyer. He knew this from an article she'd written in the *Scotsman* about domestic abuse and the law. There had been a photograph of her in which she looked more carefree than she did now.

'Are they all going on about how wonderful he was?' Susan asked. Addison was unnerved by the way she spoke to him as if she'd known him all her life. She didn't seem to expect an answer so Addison didn't give one. She tucked her hair behind her ears, a gesture that made her seem touchingly young.

'I hated him,' she said simply.

'Oh?' Addison said.

'He was a bully and a drinker. And a philanderer. I think he abused my sister, but she won't talk about it. He had no idea how to love. Love's the most important thing, you know.'

'That's what they say.'

'You think it's a sentimental cliché.'

'No. No, I don't,' Addison said. He thought about telling her that his wife had just had a baby, that they were both still in the hospital in a state of disrepair, but the whole idea of fatherhood was still so raw and unformed that he knew he would start crying if he talked about it.

Susan was holding herself as if she was very cold and suddenly every nerve and fibre and cell in Addison's body yearned to declare itself kin. Instead he said, 'Well, he's gone now,' but it came out sounding more harsh than he'd intended.

'He'll never go,' Susan said blankly. 'He'll never die. We'll carry him around inside ourselves for ever. You can't imagine what it was like to be his child.'

'No,' Addison agreed, 'I can't. I have to go,' he added awkwardly.

'Of course.'

Addison bent down and kissed Susan on the cheek. He was more surprised by this gesture than she was and, feeling oddly embarrassed, he turned up his collar against the rain and walked swiftly out of the door. The segs on his shoes struck off the York-stone slabs of the path, an echo of something he couldn't quite remember.

When he got to the gate, he looked back. Susan was still standing there, watching him.

VI

UNSEEN TRANSLATION

Αρτεμιν ἀείδω χρυσηλάκατον, κελαδεινήν,
παρθένον αἰδοίην, ἐλαφηβόλον, ἰοχέαιραν. . .

I sing of Artemis, whose shafts are of gold,
who cheers on the hounds, the pure maiden
shooter of stags, who delights in archery.

HOMERIC HYMN TO ARTEMIS

HEY HAD MANAGED AN ENTIRE AFTERNOON IN THE Bird Gallery. From egg to skeleton, from common to extinct, from flightless to free, Missy and Arthur were on familiar terms with the avian world.

'Can we come back and do mammals tomorrow?' Arthur asked.

'If you like. There are a lot of them though, remember. You might want to subdivide them into categories.'

'There were a lot of birds. We didn't subdivide them.'

'True.'

Missy believed that knowledge was best taken in small, digestible portions. Museums and galleries, in her opinion, were full of people wandering listlessly from exhibit to exhibit, their eyes glazed over with too much information and not enough knowledge.

'It's an established neurological fact,' Missy told Arthur

(Missy believed in using long words with children wherever possible), 'that window shopping and museums are the two most tiring activities for the brain. A chronic insomniac could probably come into the Natural History Museum and fall asleep before he'd got past the diplodocus in the Central Hall.' Arthur yawned.

'I've noticed you're very suggestible, Arthur.'

'Is that bad?'

'No, it's a good thing, it makes my job much easier. Just make sure it's me that you take suggestions from, not someone else.' The words 'like your mother' remained unspoken, but understood, between them.

The Natural History Museum was closing, already echoing with emptiness and a promise of the secret life it led when no one was there. Missy imagined the birds shaking out their feathers and shuffling from one stiff leg to the other, cracking neck bones and easing off flight muscles. Diplodocus himself gave a little tidal tremor along the vertebrae of his huge backbone as if warming up for a leisurely evening stroll. They took no notice of him. Missy never bothered her charges too much with dinosaurs. She thought children (not to mention parents) were far too obsessed with them already.

Outside, the threat of summer rain had darkened the South Kensington sky to an otherworldly purple.

'Are we going home?' Arthur asked, rather indifferently.

'No, we're going to Patisserie Valerie for hot chocolate and cake. Unless you don't like that idea.'

'Ha, ha.'

Missy and Arthur had spent Arthur's school holidays picking and choosing from the capital's smorgasbord of culture. This week, for example, had begun with a short visit to the British Museum (where they spent most of their time admiring Jennings Dog), followed on Tuesday by a Mozart String Quartet at the Wigmore Hall, Wednesday was Shakespeare in the Park (*As You Like It* – 'Very good' in Arthur's opinion) and yesterday it had been the eighteenth-century rooms of the National Gallery. Missy was pleased to find that Arthur was able to spend almost twenty minutes in near-silent contemplation of *Whistlejacket*. It was at that moment, as they sat companionably together considering Stubbs's huge ideal of a horse ('Essence of horse,' Missy whispered in Arthur's ear), that Missy knew for certain that Arthur was a superior version of an eight-year-old boy.

Unfortunately, children were usually spoilt for life by the time Missy got her hands on them. At two years old they had acquired all the faults that would mar them for ever and Missy had to spend most of her time rectifying their old bad habits rather than instilling new good ones. Of course, that was why Missy was called in. She had a reputation, like a Jesuitical troubleshooter, a Marine Corps Mary Poppins – when all else failed, call in Missy Clark. They expected her to drop in from the skies on the end of an umbrella, like a parachutist floating into a country in the middle of a civil war, and rescue their children from bad behaviour.

Missy was tiring of this phase of her life. She was even thinking of returning to nursing, although not to the hellish half-world of the NHS. She was considering applying to a private clinic somewhere, plastic surgery perhaps – somewhere where people weren't actually ill. If she was to remain in this job beyond the age of forty (she was thirty-eight – a difficult age) then she needed a completely blank canvas on which to practise her art. A tabula rasa, untouched by another's hand. A new baby. That was what Romney Wright had offered. A baby so untouched that it wasn't even born yet.

Missy was never interviewed by an employer, she interviewed them. Not that she was looking for the perfect family – years of experience had taught her there was no such thing. All she wanted was a family capable of reformation, and failing that, then just one child in the family who could be rescued from the fate which awaited it (ordinariness). Missy made it a rule never to stay anywhere longer than two years.

'Think of me as the SAS,' she said brightly, when the hugely pregnant Romney had engaged her two weeks before the birth of her second child. Romney – sometime wife of a rock star, glamour model and ironic game-show guest, 'now concentrating on her acting career', but mostly famous for being famous – forgot to mention the first child until Missy was dictating her non-negotiable terms and conditions (own bedroom, kitchen, bathroom and sitting room; own car; one and a half days off a week; no nights; full-time maternity nurses for the first three months; pension allowance). In fact, it was only by chance that Arthur wandered into the room at that moment and asked Romney if anyone was going to make his tea or should he heat up some baked beans? Missy was pleased at this – she liked to see a self-sufficient child and had nothing against baked beans.

'Oh, and, of course, this is Arthur,' Romney said carelessly in a grating kind of East London accent that was already beginning to annoy Missy. Hadn't elocution lessons been on the curriculum at Romney's stage school?

Missy did actually know about Arthur's existence as she had checked out Romney's (entirely tabloid) cuttings file ('My love for my little boy', 'My single-parent hell', and so on) before arriving at Romney's Primrose Hill house.

'This is the new nanny, Arthur,' Romney said.

'Oh,' Arthur said, raising surprised eyebrows. Missy liked a child who didn't speak when he had nothing to say.

'Missy,' Missy said to Arthur.

'Missy?' Romney repeated thoughtfully. 'What kind of a name is that?'

'A nickname my father gave me. It stuck.'

'Right. Well, Arthur's called Arthur because his dad was into like Camelot and all that stuff.'

'I think it's a very good name,' Missy said, smiling encouragingly at Arthur.

'It's a bit old-fashioned though, isn't it?' Romney frowned. 'I mean "Arthur Wright" sounds like your grandad or something. But that was his dad all over, thought it was funny. His dad's Campbell Wright? Lead singer with Boak? Useless piece of Scottish string. Completely debauched, the lot of them.' Romney pronounced 'debauched' with relish as if it was only recently learned. Arthur, a solemn, bespectacled boy, said nothing. Missy had already looked up Boak on the internet. Romney was surprisingly accurate in her choice of vocabulary. Boak were debauched. In photographs they all wore Second World War gas masks, so it was impossible to see if Arthur looked like his father. He certainly didn't resemble his mother, at least not in any major particular, perhaps in the whorl of an ear, the oval of a nostril, nothing too relevant.

'What would you have called him?' Missy asked, intrigued by the idea that you could be the mother of a child and not name it.

'Zeus,' Romney said, without hesitation.

'Zeus?'

'King of the gods,' Romney explained helpfully. Arthur looked at Missy with absolutely no expression on his face. Missy liked a child who kept his own counsel.

'He wears glasses, of course.' Romney sighed. 'Arthur, not Zeus, obviously. When I was a kid,' she carried on, when neither Arthur nor Missy had anything to add to this observation, 'if you wore glasses you were like "speccy four-eyes" or "double-glazing" but now it's cool, like because of Harry Potter. And that kid in that Tom Cruise film. Or no, maybe not him, I don't think that kid was cool, was he? Of course, Campbell was very romantic then, now he's a wanker, but you should have seen our wedding – he planned it all himself – in a ruined castle, I rode over the drawbridge on a white horse and when we were pronounced man and wife – although it wasn't really a vicar, it was more of a shaman kind of bloke – they released butterflies, hundreds of butterflies, over our heads. It was really something, I never thought—'

Missy stood up abruptly; she could see that Romney was a talker. 'I have to go now,' she said. 'When would you like me to start?'

'Tomorrow,' Arthur said promptly. Missy was pleased to hear that he spoke a more civilized form of the English language than his mother.

'He's a funny one, isn't he?' Romney said, for no particular reason.

Missy allowed Arthur two cakes with his hot chocolate. She understood that sometimes one simply wasn't enough.

'What do you think she'll call the baby?' Arthur asked.

'Who are we talking about – the cat's mother? Wipe your fingers.'

'You know who I mean. I bet it's something stupid.'

Romney had been delivered of a baby girl the previous day and Missy and Arthur had visited her that morning in the hospital, in the private maternity wing that was like a five-star hotel. Romney had opted to be knocked unconscious and split open rather than give birth naturally. Missy favoured natural childbirth wherever possible. She thought it was character-forming for a child to have to fight its way into existence. Missy herself was a twin and had made sure she'd elbowed her way out first, ahead of her brother.

The father of Romney's baby was a multi-millionaire, Swiss-born financier who had led an impeccably boring life until a lifelong interest in West End musicals had led him to bankroll a doomed stage version of Charlotte Brontë's *Villette* in which Romney had a small and surprisingly naked part. In a moment of champagne-and-cocaine-fuelled incontinence at the opening night party, the Swiss financier had found himself in a backstage dressing-room toilet having frantic sex with Romney – a fact which he subsequently vehemently denied when it became tabloid knowledge. ('"I am a love god!" Otto shouted in our steamy sex session.') Romney was now looking forward to the DNA tests to see just how wealthy Otto's seed would prove.

'I'm glad it's a girl,' Arthur said, finishing off his second cake (both his chosen cakes had been chocolate). 'I like girls. Do you know I used to have a male nanny once?'

'And? Was he all right?'

'So-so. He was Australian.'

'How many nannies have you had, Arthur?'

'Five. I think.'

'Why do they leave? Not because of you, you're not a difficult child.'

'Thank you.'

'What about the last one, my predecessor?'

Arthur shrugged.

'What does that mean? The shrugging?'

Arthur stood up and piled their dirty plates neatly. 'We should go. The tube's going to be packed.'

The rain held off as they walked to the underground. Missy thought it was important for a child to use public transport, to suffer dreary queues and biting winds. Even when working for the richest families she had made a point of hauling their children around the streets of London on buses and tubes and trains. She believed stoicism was a virtue that was badly in need of reviving.

They went into a newsagent's so that Missy could replenish essentials – she was never without Elastoplasts, safety pins, first-class stamps, tissues, extra-strong mints, Nurofen, cough sweets, Calpol, bottled water. The search for tissues led them past the newspaper and magazine racks which took up one wall. All of the top shelf was occupied by glossy girls presenting their buttocks or breasts to the camera.

'Difficult though it may be for you to believe, one day, sadly, you will probably find these images attractive,' Missy told Arthur. 'But for now you can buy a *Beano*.'

Arthur wasn't listening. 'Look,' he said, pointing to the rack of tabloids beneath the naked women. Nearly every newspaper had a photograph of Romney Wright on the front, posing in her hospital bed – 'Romney's bundle of joy', 'Love-rat leaves Romney holding the baby', 'Romney keeping mum about dad' (which was hardly true). Romney had managed to adopt a pose similar to the models in the pornographic magazines – her huge, milk-swollen breasts offered to the camera like gifts. The baby itself seemed incidental, almost invisible inside its shawl cocoon. Arthur skim-read the text. 'They don't mention me,' he said.

'That's a good thing.'

'I know.' Arthur gazed at the photographs of his mother as if she was an interesting stranger. 'Do you think we'll like the baby?'

'What's not to like?'

Arthur gazed at his overexposed mother. Missy liked a wise child better than anyone but she considered the expression on Arthur's face to be knowledgeable well beyond his years.

'I realize you've already had far too much chocolate today and are probably as high as a kite, which is a technical term used by nannies, but, and against my better judgement, and you will rarely hear those words from my lips, Arthur, you can have a packet of chocolate buttons. Now come on, don't dawdle.'

The baby was finally named. Romney toyed with a galaxy of goddesses ('Athene? Aphrodite? Artemis?') and gave up before reaching the end of the alphas.

'What did they do?' Arthur asked as they meandered ('from the river god Maeander, by the way') through the textile rooms of the V and A.

'Well,' Missy said, 'Athene was smug and thought she knew everything, Aphrodite was a troublemaker, and very irritating, I might add, and only Artemis had any sense.'

'What did she do?'

'Virgin, close relationship with the moon, childbirth, wolves. Oh, and the chase.'

'The chase?'

'Shot stags with silver arrows, that kind of thing.'

Arthur looked horrified. 'Shot stags?' he echoed ('from Echo – an unfortunate nymph. Show me one that isn't').

'It's a mythic thing, no stags were actually harmed during the . . . that kind of thing.'

Romney had offered the choice of name to Arthur but reneged when he opted for 'Jane', a name far too plain for Romney's tastes. In the end, she went for world geography. Romney's sister Johdi had a child called Africa and her friend Lily had a baby called India so Romney decided on China for Arthur's sister. 'Like collecting countries,' she said to Missy. 'They'll be like NATO or something when they grow up.'

'It could have been much worse,' Missy said to Arthur. 'Belgium, Luxemburg, New Zealand, Gibraltar, Uzbekistan. The list of worse is endless. That's not grammatical, by the way.'

China, although in no way Chinese, was as delicate as porcelain with creamy skin and a rosy blush on her cheeks. She was more robust than her name implied but nevertheless received round-the-clock attention from a series of maternity nurses who themselves received round-the-clock attention from the nanny-cam in the nursery. Romney had a monitor in her bedroom so that she could watch the nurse watching her baby. Otto's DNA had finally been forced to own up as the culprit ('Kraut comes clean – "China's mine" ') much to Romney's relief, although, 'He wasn't a kraut,' she said indignantly.

Autumn came. The Primrose Hill household was running smoothly – Romney was sated with money and sex, the sex in the stocky form of a soap star, Arthur was as happy as an eight-year-old boy can be at school ('OK, I suppose') and China was a dream of a child. Even the tabloid photographers had stopped camping on the doorstep and Missy was looking forward to the school break and some leaf-kicking time in London's parks with Arthur and the baby, when Romney suddenly announced that Arthur was going to visit his father for half-term.

'They have joint custody,' Arthur explained over a boiled-egg tea down in the huge basement kitchen.

'And when did you last see him?'

Arthur thought for a long time. 'Two years ago, I think. You have to come with me,' he added matter-of-factly.

'Why?'

'Because he's on tour.'

'On tour?'

'Oh yeah, didn't I say?' Romney said when Missy questioned her. 'Boak are in the middle of like this huge world tour, actually I think they're always on it. Arthur's going to visit him when they're in Germany. Flying into Munich, flying out of Hamburg at the end of the week. All the arrangements have been made by his publicist, you're going too. And I tell you what, I'm going to give you your own credit card. How's that? One more thing for the kraut to pay for.'

'He's Swiss,' Missy reminded her.

'Same difference,' Romney said.

'What about my hamster?' Arthur asked Missy.

'We'll ask Africa to look after him.'

'What about the baby?'

'It's only a week,' Missy said, 'and babies are almost indestructible, you know.' Romney, however, decided not to look after China herself but to go on a 'detox meditation' in the Cotswolds with her friend Lily while China went to stay with her maternal grandmother, who had, in Romney's words, 'been dying to get a shot at her'.

'So China will be fine,' Missy reassured Arthur. 'After all, your grandmother managed to bring your mother up.' Arthur gave Missy the most beautifully blank look.

'You can be very enigmatic sometimes, Arthur,' Missy said ('from the Greek *ainigma*, derived from *ainos* – fable').

If they were on their way to partake of Boak's debauchery, there was no indication of it in Lufthansa business class, which was so clean and grey and lacking in decadence that Arthur, a nonchalant traveller, managed to study the Collins German phrase book that Missy had bought him in an Oxfam shop prior to the trip ('Why buy new?' she said to Arthur, 'when you can buy cheap?') while Missy herself read a book about astronomy that she had taken out from the library. Missy thought it was important to use libraries. ('Why buy at all when you can borrow?') She wasn't particularly interested in astronomy but she believed an important part of her job was to impart as much general knowledge as possible to her charges, because if not her, then who?

'Did you know,' Missy asked Arthur, 'that they can weigh galaxies?'

'Sie führen mich an,' Arthur said, consulting his phrase book.

'I'm sorry?'

'You're pulling my leg,' he laughed, pleased that he knew something that Missy didn't.

Missy and Arthur were in possession of an extraordinarily detailed itinerary for the German leg of Boak's tour, prepared by the band's publicist, a girl called Lulu, who, as well as providing flight times, driver details and hotel reservations, had also given two different mobile numbers on which she could be contacted. The itinerary also informed them that they were going to travel around Germany on Boak's tour bus.

'What will that be like?' Missy asked Arthur, as the plane bumped lightly onto the runway at Munich airport. Arthur frowned, carefully searching for the right word.

'Extreme,' he said finally.

There was no car to collect them at the airport, as promised by Lulu, but Missy had changed sterling into Deutschmarks at Heathrow and they caught a taxi to the hotel with the careless abandon of people on someone else's expenses.

The Bayerischer Hof had no record of any reservation. 'Two rooms? In the name of Wright?' Missy persisted, showing the receptionist Lulu's careful itinerary. The receptionist regarded it politely as if it was a document from another civilization, far away in time and space, and beyond translation.

'Are Boak actually staying here?' Missy asked, wishing they weren't called such a stupid name. At first, the receptionist thought she was trying to say 'book' and then 'Björk'. The smile on the receptionist's face grew stiff and tired. She called the manager.

'What does boak mean, anyway?' Missy asked Arthur as they waited.

'It's Scottish for sick.'

'Ill sick or vomit sick?'

'Vomit sick.'

The manager appeared, smiling sadly, and said that he very much regretted but the hotel never revealed details about its guests. It was growing late by now and Missy felt an uncharacteristic reluctance for battle. Arthur was sitting on their luggage, looking like a weary refugee, and Missy decided they would take a room anyway. She offered the brand-new gold credit card Romney had given her before they left. A few minutes later the hotel manager returned it to her and said in a low murmur that he was very sorry but the card was 'not acceptable'. He smiled even more sadly. Missy paid for the room on her own card.

'How much money do you have?' Arthur asked.

'Quite a lot actually,' Missy said truthfully. 'I've been saving for years.'

'But you're not supposed to be paying.'

'True. But it's only for one night. I expect your father'll turn up tomorrow.'

'Das ist Pech,' Arthur consoled.

The room was nice, although not the 'luxury suite' promised by Lulu. The floors were clean and the sheets snappy with starch. Missy ordered cheese omelettes and apfelstrudel on room service. After they had eaten she phoned both the mobile numbers that Lulu had provided. One was completely dead, the other announced something impenetrable in a German that was well beyond the capacity of the phrase book. Missy phoned Romney's Primrose Hill number but there was no answer. On Romney's mobile a voice announced that it might not be switched on.

They filled in their breakfast cards – Arthur found this very exciting – and then watched an incomprehensible game show on television that even if they had been fluent in German they probably wouldn't have understood. They went to their beds at nine o'clock German time, eight o'clock Primrose Hill time, and they both slept as soundly as babies until the maid hammered on the door with their breakfast, long after the dawn had scattered her yellow robes across the skies.

After breakfast, which Arthur liked almost as much as the ordering of it, Missy tried all the phone numbers she had tried the previous evening, with the same result. 'Es sind schlechte Zeiten,' Arthur said, leafing industriously through his phrase book. 'Wie schade.'

Missy went down to reception and looked the sadly smiling manager in the eye in the same way that she looked at little boys when she particularly wanted them to tell her the truth.

'If you were me,' she said to him, 'and think about this carefully, would you stay another night in this unbelievably expensive hotel and wait for the band known, unfortunately, as Boak to turn up?'

'No,' he said, 'I wouldn't.'

'Thank you.'

'Look at it this way,' Missy said to Arthur. 'Our flight from Hamburg isn't for another week, we have enough money – even if it's mine – and we are in one of the great cultural cities of Western Europe in the half-term holidays, so we may as well enjoy ourselves.'

They moved into a guest house on Karlstrasse, although they returned several times to the Bayerischer Hof to check that Boak hadn't suddenly materialized. 'Hat jemand nach uns gefragt?' Arthur asked the sad manager. No, he replied, in English, they hadn't.

They trekked to the Olympiahalle and discovered a tour poster slashed with a banner in large red capitals, declaring that Boak's concert was 'Entfällt'.

'I think that means cancelled,' Arthur said without

bothering to consult the German dictionary they'd bought ('Sometimes you have no choice but to buy'). After that, they didn't bother returning to the Bayerischer Hof. Lulu and Romney remained unreachable by all means.

'Perhaps we're dead,' Arthur suggested, 'and we just don't know it.'

'I think that's a rather fanciful explanation,' Missy said.

In accord with Missy's beliefs, they visited museums and galleries in moderation – the Forum der Technik (but only the Planetarium), the Deutsches Museum (but only the coal mine), the Alte Pinakothek (but only pre-sixteenth-century paintings). Arthur stayed awake for the whole of the BMW museum – he wasn't an eight-year-old boy for nothing – but was asleep on his feet within minutes of going into the Residenz-Museum. The Frauenkirche and the Peterskirche had much the same effect on both of them. An expedition to the Schloss Nymphenburg might have been more of a success if it hadn't rained so much. Their favourite museum exhibit was a chance discovery, a stuffed creature, in the oddly named Jagd- und Fischereimuseum ('Hunting and fishing,' Arthur supplied helpfully). The 'Wolpertinger' was a curious Mitteleuropean chimera, a mix of rabbit, stag and duck, plus something less definable and more frightening. ('Distantly related to the rare wolfkin,' Missy said.)

'Bavarian primeval creature,' Arthur read from the guide-book the sad hotel manager had given them on their last visit to the Bayerischer Hof.

In truth, neither of them was much in the mood for history and culture and they spent a lot of time wandering in the Englischer Garten or drinking hot chocolate. Every day at midday they went and stood ritualistically in front of the glockenspiel on the Neues Rathaus and watched for all the brightly coloured figures to make their rounds.

'What did happen to your last nanny?' Missy asked as they waited for the glockenspiel to start. Arthur made a pinched sort of face.

'What,' Missy encouraged, 'she was murdered? She killed herself, she came back as a ghost and wandered round a lake? Fell in love with the master who had a mad wife in the attic and who became hideously disfigured in a fire?'

'You're not supposed to talk like that to eight-year-olds.'

'Sorry.'

'She left.'

'Left?'

'Left. She said she wouldn't leave and she did. And I liked her.' Arthur stuck his hands in his pockets and angrily kicked an imaginary stone on the ground. 'I liked her and she promised she wouldn't leave and she did. And you'll leave.' His face began to quiver and he kicked the ground harder. His shoe was getting scuffed. Missy tried to touch the small shoulders, heaving with suppressed tears, but Arthur grew suddenly hysterical and shook her off.

'You'll leave just like she did,' he screamed. 'You'll leave me and I hate you! I hate you, I hate you, I hate you!'

'Arthur—'

'Shut up, shut up, shut up!' he yelled, so wound up now that he could hardly breathe, and several passers-by regarded with curiosity the small English boy struggling furiously to escape his mother's grip.

'It feels as though we've been away years,' Arthur said when the cab dropped them off at Munich airport.

'I know.'

'Do you think anyone's missed us?'

'Can you see the Lufthansa sales desk?'

'Over there.'

Arthur, Missy was relieved to see, was quite calm today, although his eyes were still red from crying – he had sobbed for hours, long after Missy had got him back to the Karlstrasse guest house, long after she had put him to bed with milk and honey cake offered by the sympathetic proprietress. 'Die Kinder,' she sighed, as if to be a child was the worst thing in the world. Arthur had finally fallen asleep, flushed and tear-stained, clutching onto Missy's hand. 'I don't hate you, you know,' he said, with a grief-stricken hiccup. 'I love you really.'

'I love you too,' she said, kissing the top of his head, 'and I promise I won't leave you and I never break promises. Ever. You'll leave me one day, though,' she added softly when Arthur was asleep.

*

They waited in the queue at the ticket sales desk. The airport was hot and incredibly busy. So many airlines, so many destinations. Arthur read them off the departure board: 'Paris, Rome, Lisbon, New York, London Heathrow.'

'I think we should have bought these tickets earlier,' Missy said, looking uncharacteristically distracted. Arthur yawned extravagantly. 'Ich langweile mich,' he said. 'At least I learnt some German.'

'Yes, you've done very well, Arthur,' Missy said vaguely.

'Are you all right?'

'Mm.'

The Lufthansa sales clerk regarded Missy's request for two single tickets to Hamburg with solemnity. She would gladly sell her them, she said, but all the Hamburg flights were full until that evening, did she still want to go?

'How about London?' Missy asked.

'I can get you on the next flight to Heathrow,' the sales clerk said, 'but not sitting together.'

'It will be quicker for us just to go straight home,' Missy said to Arthur.

'Mm,' Arthur said.

Missy thought about buying a ticket for London. She thought for rather a long time so that the sales clerk grew agitated because of the long queue snaking and coiling and knotting behind Arthur and Missy.

'Arthur,' Missy said finally, 'have you ever been to Rome?'

'I don't think so.'

'I can get you on a connecting flight to Rome leaving in half an hour,' the sales clerk said hopefully.

'A lot of museums in Rome,' Arthur said.

'A lot,' Missy agreed.

'And there are other places too,' Arthur said.

'Oh, yes,' Missy agreed, 'there are many places. So many places that you need never come back to where you started from.'

'Which was Primrose Hill,' Arthur said. He tugged at Missy's hand. 'What about China?'

'China?' the sales clerk asked, looking agitated.

'Don't panic,' Missy said to her ('from the Great God Pan, now dead, thank goodness'). 'I don't know about China,' Missy said solemnly to Arthur. 'I'm afraid her fate may be to stay with Romney.'

'You're going to have to hurry,' the sales clerk said, 'the gate will be closing soon.'

They ran. They ran so fast Arthur was sure they were going to take off before they even got on the plane. Missy pulled him along by the hand and when he looked at her feet her sensible leather boots had turned into silver sandals and he wondered if that was why they were able to run so fast. The airport tannoy stopped announcing that passengers for Düsseldorf should go to the gate and instead broadcast the rousing sound of a hunting horn. For a few dizzy seconds

Arthur saw the quiver of silver arrows on Missy's back, gleaming with moonshine. He saw her green, wolfish eyes light up with amusement as she shouted, 'Come on, Arthur, hurry up,' while a pack of hounds bayed and boiled around her silver-sandalled feet, eager for the chase.

VII

EVIL DOPPELGÄNGERS

All that we see or seem
Is but a dream within a dream

EDGAR ALLAN POE, 'A DREAM WITHIN A DREAM'

THAT WAS A PRETTY GOOD NIGHT ON SATURDAY, Fielding,' Joshua said cheerfully.

'Yeah,' Fielding said, concentrating on getting coffee from the pot into his mug. Fielding's hand seemed to have developed an unnerving tremor, which he thought was probably something to do with alcoholic poisoning. The last thing he felt like was a chummy round-the-coffee-machine-chat with Josh whateverhisnameis at this time on a Monday morning. It was considered etiquette in the Features department not to talk unnecessarily before 11.00 a.m. but Josh was new and seemed wilfully ignorant of all the rules.

'I was wrecked,' Joshua persisted. 'Not as wrecked as you though.' He laughed. 'You were completely out of it, I'm surprised you got home.'

'Yeah.' There was something fresh-faced and bouncy

about Joshua that reminded Fielding of a *Blue Peter* presenter and which was unwelcome at this, or indeed any, time of day. Fielding's head was pounding. He didn't think it was possible to have such a bad headache and not be in the middle of a brain haemorrhage. Perhaps he *was* in the middle of a brain haemorrhage. That might account for the fact that the last thing he could remember before waking up this morning was a round of end-of-the-week cocktails in the bar round the corner from the newspaper's offices. But surely that was Friday? What had happened to Saturday and Sunday? He downed his coffee quickly and poured another.

Joshua had shadowed Fielding for his first couple of weeks on the paper and still seemed irritatingly attracted to Fielding's orbit. Fielding was grudgingly grateful for Josh's existence though, because it meant that, on the last-in-first-out principle, he himself was no longer the newest member of the department.

Fielding, although nominally the media correspondent, had written hardly anything else but the TV review column since he'd joined the paper. At first he thought being the TV critic would be a cool job. He'd envisaged it as an opportunity to watch endless re-runs of *Buffy* and *Star Trek: Voyager* and write witty post-ironic little essays on television and culture ('Levi-Straussian character function in *EastEnders*', '*ER* – High Mimetic or Low Mimetic?'), recycled from his (now rather old) Media Studies degree, but instead it had turned out to be a relentless diet of worthy documentaries, savage nature programmes and mediocre two-part police procedurals.

'I couldn't believe it when you did that thing with Russell's car—'

'Yeah. It was a riot. Excuse me, Josh—'

'Joshua.'

'Whatever. I just have to go and . . .' Fielding gestured vaguely behind him.

'Yeah, me too,' Joshua said. 'I've got that piece to write up about *Green Acres*.'

'Oh?' Fielding said, trying to sound casual. 'What piece about *Green Acres*?'

'Big piece for the Saturday supplement that Flavia asked me to do.'

'Oh?'

'Yeah, I was up there last week on set, doing cast interviews and stuff for the big all-week special that's coming up. I think you were busy with that lottery winners makeover thing. Romney Wright made a guest appearance.'

'Did you meet her?' Fielding asked, his intellect suddenly suppressed by testosterone.

'Yes,' Joshua said. 'She was a very nice person.'

'With huge breasts?'

Joshua looked uncomfortable, 'That's not how we should define women, Fielding.'

'Yes, but huge breasts – yes or no?'

'Yes.'

'Is she really going to give birth live on the internet?'

'That's a ridiculous idea. Anyhoo, *Green Acres* – any thoughts about how I should approach it?'

'No.' As if he would help Josh. Fielding tried to think, but his brain felt bruised and a vulture appeared to be pecking at his liver. He should have been the one to do the *Green Acres* piece. How would he ever get out of the ghetto of TV criticism if Flavia had developed a preference for Josh whateverhisnameis over him? For some reason, Fielding's father's Conservative Club vocabulary jumped in to help out his own ailing lexicon and 'little whippersnapper' were the words that came to his mind.

'Well,' Joshua said, 'must get to work.'

'Hey, Josh!' Fielding shouted after Joshua's purposeful, retreating back.

'It's Joshua!' Joshua shouted back with a big goofy smile on his face.

'What *did* I do to Russell's car?'

'God, you're really funny, Fielding,' Joshua laughed.

Fielding went and shut himself in a cupboard. Officially the cupboard was called the viewing room but that gave it a dignity above its station. It contained a television, a video recorder and an upright chair on which it was impossible to get comfortable – which Fielding supposed was the point, otherwise every slacker in the building would have been snoozing away in there. Although the viewing room had the air of a bloodless torture chamber, it was the one place, apart from the toilet cubicles, where Fielding could get some respite from the aggressively open-plan office. Not even senior editors had their own office, a policy that was supposed to foster 'democracy and trust', but which in reality meant that the diversions that made labouring on a computer all day bearable for Fielding – endless games of Solitaire and Mah-Jong, online gambling, the regular visits to porn web-cam sites and *Buffy* chat rooms – were now out of bounds unless he wanted to become the object of censure or, worse, derision.

Flavia herself sat in the centre of the office, claiming that this made her 'always available'. Fielding was reminded of an unbelievably ugly spider he had watched on some nature documentary, squatting in the middle of its web, waiting for the arrival of hapless prey.

The rest of the newspaper occupied the glass-and-air upper floors but for some reason Features was consigned to the Tartarus-like depths of the earth. Lit only by artificial daylight and always hot and airless, the Features department was, Fielding imagined, like that desolate area around the entrance to Hades that was populated by all the bad abstract nouns, such as Fear and Grief, Anxiety, Agony and Hunger. Fielding was on first-name terms with them all, especially the last. He hadn't had any breakfast since – when? He was starving. Had he eaten at all on his lost weekend?

Fielding took a tape out of the padded brown envelope delivered ten minutes earlier by a bike courier and put it into the video's slot, which made him think of toast, which reminded him how hungry he was. He watched ten minutes of the tape – some historical-medical-detective thing, *Silent Witness* meets *The House of Eliott* piece of crap (*The Secret Life of Jemima Bates*) – and despite the hardness of the chair, fell asleep.

When he woke up he found that the plot didn't seem to have moved on at all but time had been measured by a snail-trail of drool that had crept down his chin. He only woke up at all because the door of the cupboard was flung open by Gwen Anderson, who gave Fielding a disgusted look and said, 'For God's sake, Fielding, you look repulsive.'

'Some of us are ill,' Fielding said. Fielding wondered why no one ever took any notice of the 'Do Not Disturb' sign he had pinned to the door. Gwen had curly hair and for an unnerving moment all the curls turned into little snakes that writhed and coiled on her head.

'Bad hair day?' Fielding said.

'What?'

Fielding supposed he was hallucinating from hunger. He suspected he was going to throw up and was intensely relieved when Gwen didn't engage him in further conversation but left abruptly, slamming the door on purpose so that Fielding winced and gave out an involuntary whimper of pain. Groaning quietly, he got up from the chair and picked his way across the floor as delicately as a new-born deer, in case his head fell off. He took the tape out of the video and stuffed it in his bag. He really needed to go somewhere and lie down.

Flavia had her back to Fielding and was bawling at some hapless minion and Fielding used this opportunity to try to skulk past her Black Widow bulk before she noticed him.

'That "pretending you're invisible" thing doesn't actually work, Fielding,' Gwen murmured to him as he crept by her desk. Fielding made an obscene gesture at her; she made one back. Fielding liked to imagine they were indulging in sophisticated foreplay but deep down he suspected that she might really loathe him.

'Going so soon, Fielding?' Flavia barked suddenly, without even turning round. He supposed she had sensed the vibrations on her web. 'It seems like you only just got here,' she said, spinning round in her chair. Fielding caught a whiff of her strident perfume. She checked her watch in a theatrical fashion. 'Oh, look, you *have* only just got here.'

Working from home was a perfectly acceptable practice and yet Flavia treated it as a sign of the kind of weakness that might easily lead to you being fired. Fielding waved a piece of paper in the air. He had worked in enough newspaper offices to know that waving a piece of paper around in an important fashion usually fooled people into thinking you were on a mission. 'Got to research a few things,' he said to Flavia.

'Ah, the old "waving the piece of paper" trick,' Gwen laughed. Fielding gave her a black look.

'I do have to,' Fielding protested sincerely to Flavia, so sincerely that he almost believed it himself, and when he got home he started playing *Jemima Bates* again from the beginning on the television at the foot of his bed. This time, the opening credits hadn't even finished rolling before Fielding was sound asleep on top of the covers.

'Hi, Fielding.'

'Hi, Nina.'

Nina was Flavia's PA, one of those neat, capable sort of girls who were never attracted to Fielding. Nina had French-manicured nails and a precision-cut sixties bob and no sense of humour. Fielding's heart sank as he saw her approaching his desk because the only time she ever did this was to convey some ludicrous 'bright idea' for an article from Flavia (why couldn't she use e-mail like everyone else?), nearly always on the topic of reality TV ('It's the future, Fielding'). Would Fielding, for example, like to spend a week as an inmate in the new Second World War prisoner-of-war camp reality show (*Pow!*)? Would he be a contestant on a show where you were locked up for a month with ten other people and vied to see who could put on the most weight for a huge cash prize (*Porkie Pie*)? Fielding had managed to avoid all of these 'bright ideas' so far but he knew it was only a matter of time before Flavia forced him to partake in some deeply embarrassing public ordeal in which some, if not all, of his character weaknesses would be revealed (cowardice, intolerance, complete lack of musical talent – to name just a few).

Fielding had mugged up the symptoms of several sudden-onset illnesses in case of this eventuality and was quite prepared to go as far as an emergency appendectomy if it helped him to avoid ritual humiliation. Fielding had once pointed out to Flavia that he was someone who had served as a Bafta judge. 'This is a broadsheet, Flavia, I'm a serious journalist.'

'So?' she had said. 'What's your point?'

'Nina,' Fielding said in a business-like way, picking up a piece of paper from his desk and standing up. 'Can this wait?' He waved the piece of paper. 'It's just I've got to see this.'

A shadow of confusion, swiftly followed by one of disappointment, passed over Nina's face. 'Oh, right, sure,' she said. 'It was just that I, um . . . I wanted – I thought maybe . . .' This didn't sound like one of Flavia's precise edicts. Nina, no longer merely an intermediary, seemed to be speaking, rather badly, with her own words. Fielding was astonished to see a blush, like rosy-fingered dawn, creep up her neck and spread out over her face. He was intrigued.

'Go on,' he coaxed. 'What did you think?'

Nina chewed her lip, rubbing away at the shiny pink lip-gloss she always wore. Fielding found himself strangely transfixed by Nina's lips. He couldn't take his eyes off them – they were perfect. In fact, all of Nina's features, when he looked at them, were just right, neither too small nor too big, unlike Flavia who had had her lips injected with collagen and now resembled a puffer fish. Flavia also had regular Botox injections, so that more and more she looked as if she was wearing her own death mask. Nina's features, on the other hand, were untouched by artifice. Fielding thought of milkmaids and meadows. He wondered if he was coming down with something.

'It's OK,' Nina said, indicating the piece of paper. 'You're busy.'

Fielding put the piece of paper back on the desk. 'It can wait,' he said.

'I just wanted to say thank you,' Nina said, smiling at him.

'For?' Fielding said.

'For last night.'

'Last night,' Fielding echoed. Fielding sensed this was delicate. If he indicated that he had no idea what she was talking about she would stalk off but if he didn't know what he'd done . . . what had he done last night? Surely he'd fallen asleep in front of *Jemima Bates*?

'Monday night?' he said brightly.

'No, last night, Tuesday.' Nina was still smiling at

him, waiting for a more meaningful response.

'Today's Wednesday?'

'Yes, Fielding.' He could sense that she was losing patience with him. He'd lost another day? Was he drinking so much that he was beginning to have regular blackouts?

'Yeah, right, Nina, sorry, it's just I've had a bit of flu.'

'You seemed all right last night,' Nina said. 'More than all right in fact.' She giggled. Had he had sex with Nina? And he couldn't remember? How unlikely was that? Perhaps he had some kind of brain tumour that was affecting his memory?

'I had a wonderful time,' Nina said. There was definitely a hint of innuendo in that strangely humourless giggle of hers.

'Really?' Fielding said. He laughed in a suave kind of way that suggested he was used to sexual compliments.

Nina giggled again. 'You know, the funny thing,' she continued blithely, 'is that we always thought you were gay.'

Fielding took a moment to digest this idea. 'We?' he said eventually.

'Well, you know,' Nina said, tossing her bobbed head in the direction of the entire office. He could see two women with whom he'd had sex. Enthusiastic, albeit drunken, sex. Heterosexual sex nonetheless.

Fielding frowned. 'I'm not,' he said. 'I'm not gay.'

'I know that now, silly,' Nina laughed.

'So, Nina,' Fielding said, deciding that he might as well

make the most of this mysterious conquest, 'do you want to see me again? Dinner maybe? Tonight?'

Nina looked surprised and absurdly flattered. 'That would be nice, Fielding.'

'Right, I'll pick you up about . . . seven thirty?'

'Great.'

Fielding swung by the water cooler, feeling invigorated if puzzled. He took one of the small Dixie cups that reminded him of a mental hospital, or probably a mental hospital in a film because he didn't recollect ever having been inside a real mental hospital. But who knows, he thought to himself. Now that it appeared he was leading a double life, who knew what he had been up to?

He suddenly realized that he'd drunk at least six cups of water. He had a raging thirst that seemed impossible to slake. He downed several more cups. He would like to have taken one back with him to his desk but they were the stupid conical ones – what was the point of a cup you couldn't put down?

'Hey, Russell,' Fielding said as Russell strode in the door, hefting cameras and camera equipment. He had the air of a man who'd just come back from a strenuous military expedition although he was only a sports photographer.

'Tell me,' Fielding said, full of camaraderie, 'what's the point of a cup if you can't put it down?'

'Is that a riddle?' Russell asked, glaring aggressively at

Fielding. Fielding backed away a little. Russell lowered his voice to a menacing growl. 'I don't know how you dare even fucking speak to me, Fielding, after what you did to my car.'

'Yeah,' Fielding said and dived into the lift. 'Gotta go, Russ.' Fielding pushed the button for the top floor. There were several conference rooms on the top floor, usually empty, and Fielding often went up for a wander round as an antidote to the underworld where he worked. The lift was notoriously slow and he waited patiently in an army at-ease stance, or at least a civilian's approximation of one. Fielding had been told by Greg, one of the security men, that there was a hidden CCTV camera in the lift and although he didn't know if this was true or not Fielding always made a point of behaving impeccably in case Flavia ever looked at the tapes.

Fielding found an empty room with a sofa in it, lay down, and fell asleep.

When he returned to Features he found that half the staff, including Flavia, had gone to a seminar on 'The Media in the Digital Age', so he decided to leave early. Nina wasn't at her desk either. 'If you're looking for Little Miss Butter-wouldn't-melt,' Gwen said, 'she's gone to pick up Flavia's kids from school.'

'Is that part of her job?'

'It is if Flavia says it is. She asked me to do it the other day. Imagine. Cheeky cow. So,' she added with a sneer, 'I hear you're really hot in the sack, Fielding.'

Fielding shrugged nonchalantly. 'What can I say, Gwen?' He tipped an imaginary hat and left the office, whistling.

On his way out, Fielding bumped into Crawford and, as surreptitiously as possible, made an archaic gesture to ward off the evil eye, taught him by an ex-girlfriend. Although she hadn't so much taught it to him as done it to him. Crawford was in charge of Obituaries, a fact which Fielding found unsettling, although not as unsettling as the way Crawford nurtured his old-fogeyness, dressing in check suits and mustard waistcoats and sporting a gold fob-watch which he frequently pulled out and gazed at as if consulting an oracle.

'Leaving us so soon, Mr Fielding?' he asked pleasantly. Fielding had long since given up explaining to Crawford that Fielding was his first name – Crawford's inability to grasp even this simple fact made him seem particularly unsuitable for the job he was in.

'Working at home,' Fielding said.

Crawford peered at him from over his little half-moon spectacles. 'You look dreadful.'

'Thank you.'

'You look as though you've spent the night strapped to the winged and fiery wheel.'

'Yeah, something like that.' Fielding rarely had any idea what Crawford was talking about.

Crawford consulted his watch and then gestured at the

huge tree that dominated the glass atrium. Fielding frequently pondered the logistics of this tree. How had they got it there? Had they lowered it on a crane or simply built the offices around it? Flavia claimed it was a postmodern statement but how a tree could be postmodern was beyond Fielding.

'The Elm of False Dreams,' Crawford sighed mysteriously.

'I think it's a sycamore,' Fielding said. 'I think all the elms are dead.'

'How sad,' Crawford said. 'And now, if you'll excuse me, I must go and write Romney Wright's obituary.'

'She's dead?'

'Not at all. Just in case. You never know with her sort.'

Fielding didn't even make it to the coffee machine the next morning before Nina was onto him like a Harpy. She slapped his face so hard that he thought he might have whiplash. Tears of pain stung his eyes.

'Fucking hell, Nina,' he spluttered, 'what was that about?'

'Like you don't know?' she shouted at him, her mouth now far from perfect as it distorted itself into a hideous kind of grin. 'You are the most disgusting man I have ever known,' she said. 'You're a reptile, jail would be too good for you.' No one in the office was even pretending to work, they were all transfixed by this thrilling real-life soap. Nina started sobbing and Fielding made an instinctive move to comfort her. She started screaming.

Gwen came over and put an arm around Nina. All the little snakes on her head hissed at Fielding as she led Nina away. 'Fucking hell, Fielding,' Gwen said over her shoulder. 'What did you *do* to her?'

Fielding contemplated his reflection in the mirror in the men's room. His cheek was branded with a livid red handprint that looked as if it would never fade. Perhaps he'd be marked for ever as a punishment for whatever it was he'd done. Was there a rogue Fielding out there, playing havoc with his life? What was the last thing he could remember? Fielding frowned at his mirrored self. He remembered going home. He had a vague memory of looking through his wardrobe, deciding what to wear for his date with Nina and then – nothing. Total amnesia. Was that a Schwarzenegger film? Maybe he was concussed. Or brainwashed.

Joshua came into the men's room. 'Blimey, Fielding,' he said, 'what happened to you?' Fielding hadn't thought there was anyone left who still said 'blimey'. 'What did you do – join the Red Hand Gang?' Joshua laughed – rather a lot – at his joke.

'You missed the fracas then?' Fielding sighed.

'Fracas? What fracas? Have you been up to your tricks again, Fielding?'

Fielding peered closely into the mirror. He looked perfectly normal – his eyes a little more bloodshot than usual perhaps, his skin a little pale, but on the whole he looked like himself. 'Josh?'

'Joshua,' Joshua corrected pleasantly.

'Can you think of a reason why someone would forget hours and hours of their life? Forget what they'd been doing in that time?'

'Like sleepwalking, you mean?'

'Sleepwalking, of course!' Fielding said. How reasonable that sounded. 'Brilliant, Josh, thanks.' Fielding left the men's room, feeling suddenly jaunty. Which was a Josh kind of word, he thought.

'It's Joshua,' Joshua said quietly to the mirror.

Fielding was ravenous. He couldn't remember a time now when he hadn't been hungry. He thought he must have some kind of metabolic disease, perhaps one of its side effects was loss of memory. Fielding took a tuna melt as well as a ham and cheese ploughman's into the viewing room and settled down with a *Green Acres* tape. The *Green Acres* week-long special involved a petrol-tanker crash, a wedding in which the bride of Digby Craddock, the shepherd, turned out to be a transvestite, and a subplot in which Veronica Steer, the village postmistress, suspected a young thug of sheep rustling. *Green Acres* wouldn't be *Green Acres* without an underlying narrative device about sheep. Fielding made a note of that sentence, it would make a good opening line for his review. He wondered if Joshua had interviewed any sheep when he was in the sticks doing his *Green Acres* special. Was it sticks, or was it Styx? Was the Styx the river that made you forget everything? Or was that Lethe?

'Are you all right?' A tall girl was frowning at him. Fielding racked his brains – a journalism student, on a work placement, frighteningly clever. Sarah? Hannah?

'It says "Do Not Disturb" on the door,' Fielding said to her, through a mouthful of cheese and pickle.

'It always says that.'

'Maybe it always means it. Did you want something? Sarah?'

'Emma. I just wanted to say thank you to you actually.'

Fielding groaned and slapped his forehead with his palm. 'Oh God, I didn't have sex with you, did I?'

Emma looked at him in horror. 'Is that some kind of joke?'

'Yes,' Fielding said quickly, 'and a very bad one. Sorry. What was it that I actually helped you with?' Fielding tried to sound offhand but not-remembering produced a physical pain in his head. His stomach gave out a huge groaning rumble. How could he be hungry at the same time as he was eating?

Emma frowned at him in the same primary-school-teacher way that Gwen did. Where did they breed these scary girls? Some kind of Amazonian boarding school in the Home Counties?

'The piece on *Buffy*,' Emma said. 'I wouldn't have been able to do it without your unbelievable knowledge . . .'

Fielding preened a little.

'. . . of trivia,' Emma concluded.

'And you're sure it was me who helped you?' Fielding asked, although without too much hope. It seemed unlikely anyone else in the office, even Joshua, could match Fielding in the Buffy stakes.

'Yes, I am sure it was you, Fielding. Mind you, I have to say,' Emma added thoughtfully, 'you did seem different yesterday.'

'Different? How?'

'I don't know. Smarter. Less of an airhead. All that stuff about Kant's theories of the noumenal and phenomenal self and how it relates to the Slayer. Quite impressive.'

'Thanks.'

'Shame you're such a prick.'

'Thanks.'

Fielding had imagined that it might be difficult to fall asleep with the voyeuristic eye of the camera on him but within minutes of setting up the CCTV system lent to him by Greg, Fielding was dead to the world and only woke up when the alarm shrilled in his ear. Armed with strong coffee, he settled down to watch the tape, eager for any evidence of somnambulation. Even on fast forward, Fielding's night was remarkably boring, almost worse than watching *Jemima Bates*, which, he remembered with a twitch of guilt, aired tomorrow and he still hadn't written a review for it. Fielding was surprised to see what a restless sleeper he was – tossing and turning all night long as if plagued by demons. But he never left the bed, not once.

He phoned Joshua. 'Josh, did you see me last night, did we go out?'

Josh laughed. 'We certainly did, we went—'

'Thanks.' Fielding put the phone down. So, now he knew that the 'other Fielding', as he thought of him, was not his sleeping self. Fielding racked his brains for an explanation that was within the bounds of reason. Identical twins? Fielding had once dated an identical twin but had found the whole concept freakish. He didn't see that there was much difference between having an identical twin and having a doppelgänger. He phoned his mother. He knew she would already be breakfasted, groomed and coiffed and sitting in her cashmere and pearls wondering what to do for the rest of the day.

'Fielding,' she said when she picked up the phone. 'You're up early.'

Fielding tried to sound as if he was asking an everyday kind of question. 'I didn't have an identical twin that you had adopted at birth, did I?'

There was a surprised clink of ice cubes on the other end of the phone. Did his mother really start on the gin this early in the morning? For a giddy moment Fielding thought his mother was going to answer in the affirmative but then heard her take a discreet swig before saying, rather cautiously, 'I don't think so, Fielding.'

*

Fielding skirted warily round the outskirts of the office trying to keep as far away as possible from Nina, Gwen, Emma or Flavia. (When exactly was it decided that the world was going to be run by women? Fielding had obviously missed that meeting.) He settled himself at his desk and industriously opened e-mails, drinking three lattes one after the other while eating his way through a bag of Starbucks muffins.

'Hungry?' Joshua laughed.

'Always,' Fielding said.

'So, Fielding – last night was a bit of a blur, was it? How did you get on?' Joshua asked, with what looked suspiciously like a smirk.

'Slept like a baby,' Fielding said, keeping his eyes on the screen to discourage Joshua's relentless bonhomie.

'Really?' Joshua sounded astonished. 'I would have thought that stripper would have kept you up all night.'

'Stripper?'

'Well, OK,' Joshua said, 'lap dancer, but same difference really, isn't it?'

'Stripper?'

'The one you went home with. From Bottoms Up. The show bar.'

Fielding leapt up from his desk and grabbed Joshua by the arm. He steered him into the viewing room and pushed him into the chair.

'Josh—'

'Joshua.'

'Listen carefully. I was not in a show bar with you last night.'

'Oh, I see,' Joshua laughed. 'It's OK, your secret's safe with me.'

'No, no, no. Listen.' Fielding spoke slowly as if to an idiot. 'I wasn't there.'

'I'm not surprised you can't remember. I've never seen anyone knock back White Russians like that.'

'I don't drink White Russians.'

'You did last night.'

'No – it was someone else, someone who looks like me. I, me, Fielding Carter, was not in that club with you last night.'

'Where were you then?'

'Asleep in my bed.' Fielding took the CCTV tape and thrust it into the video. 'Watch,' he said to Josh.

Joshua watched in silence for a few seconds. 'You video yourself sleeping, Fielding?' he said, puzzled.

'Not usually.'

'Is this some kind of reality TV?'

'No, it *is* reality, Josh,' Fielding said, 'real reality. See the date on it, see the time on it? I'm sleeping *at the same time as* I'm in the show bar. Watch while I fast forward.'

'OK, OK. But you could have falsified the date on the tape.'

'What possible reason could I have for wanting to doctor this tape?'

'So, what are you saying, Fielding?' Joshua frowned. 'You think you have a double?'

'What other explanation is there?' an agitated Fielding demanded. 'How else could I be in two places at once?'

'Identical twins separated at birth?' Joshua hazarded.

'No, my mother doesn't think so.'

'She's not sure?'

'Never mind,' Fielding said dismissively. 'Any other reasons?'

'There's a parallel universe with another Fielding in it,' Joshua offered. 'Another Joshua. Another Flavia. Another Gwen. Another Russell—'

'Yeah, yeah, I get the idea,' Fielding said impatiently.

'Temporal anomaly – they happen in *Voyager* all the time.'

'Anything else?'

'A clone?'

'Doubtful,' Fielding said.

'Oh, I know,' Joshua said eagerly, 'it's like that Hans Christian Andersen story where the guy's shadow takes over his life and then has him killed.'

'Likely or not?'

'Not,' Joshua admitted. 'You're insane?'

'Possible,' Fielding conceded. 'But I don't feel insane, although of course I don't know what insane feels like. Maybe it feels like normal?'

'Paranoid and delusional?'

'Almost certainly. It doesn't alter the fact that there's

someone out there who looks just like me and is living my life, only apparently with more success.'

'That's like in *Buffy*,' Joshua said enthusiastically, 'when Xander had a double, which was played by his real-life identical twin, of course—'

'Yeah, yeah, I know and it turned out Xander was split in two and the two halves couldn't live without each other. I really don't think that's what's happened.'

'There only seems to be one answer then,' Joshua said. 'You have a doppelgänger. It happens all the time.'

'It does?'

The viewing room was becoming increasingly claustrophobic. Fielding opened the door and started walking towards his desk, Joshua at his heels like an enthusiastic sheepdog.

'I mean there are endless metaphorical implications,' Joshua rambled on. 'The two sides of the self, good and evil, and so on. It's the whole basis of *Buffy* – evil Willow, robot Buffy, when Buffy and Faith change places, all the stuff with Ben and Glory—'

'Josh!' Fielding was surprised to hear himself yelling. People in the office stopped work and looked at him. Fielding took a deep breath to calm himself. 'Josh, I never thought I would ever say this but – Buffy isn't real.'

Joshua laughed and looked around the Features department. 'And you think this is real, Fielding?' He loped off, still laughing.

'Ah, Mr Fielding,' Crawford said, suddenly appearing at Fielding's side, 'look at it.'

'Look at what?'

Crawford swept a hand around in the air in a grand gesture that encompassed the entire room. 'The Plain of Judgement and the Vale of Mourning.'

'Crawford?'

'Yes?'

'Piss off, would you?'

'My pleasure.'

'Fielding!'

'Christ, Flavia, you'll give someone a heart attack sneaking up like that.'

Flavia looked at him with distaste. 'Have you written that *Jemima Bates* review yet?'

'Almost finished.'

'You look like hell, Fielding.'

'I haven't been myself recently.'

Fielding took the *Jemima Bates* tape into the viewing room. He had lost count of how many times he had started to watch it and fallen asleep. It was like some dreadful Sisyphean task he had been set. Fielding wondered what the other Fielding was doing. Undoubtedly having more fun than this Fielding was. Was it possible for only one of them to be active at any one time? Perhaps it was like matter and anti-matter and the two Fieldings (strangely, Fielding had begun to think of his double as an equal) couldn't exist at the same time. What was his doppelgänger up to, Fielding wondered? Was its goal to get rid of the original and take his place? Or simply to destroy his life? Whom the gods punish they first make mad, wasn't that what they said?

Fielding woke up in the dark. The last thing he remembered was Jemima Bates scurrying through the back alleys of Victorian London, looking for the perpetrator of some dastardly crime while being pursued by a shadowy figure. Fielding wondered what time it was. The familiar illuminated dial of his bedside clock was dark. Perhaps there had been a power cut. Fielding was incredibly cold and uncomfortable. He looked around him. He was lying in an alley.

Fielding lay very still for a while, hoping that he was hallucinating, and only moved when forced to by the appearance of a mangy feral dog sniffing around his head. For an awful moment Fielding thought it had three heads. He'd occasionally seen double after a rough night, but never triple. Thankfully, the three heads resolved into one.

Fielding ached all over. Apart from his usual raging hunger and thirst, his head was pounding with the worst kind of hangover headache. A pool of vomit – possibly his own – proved attractive to the dog. Fielding stumbled to his feet. His mouth tasted of brass and a fur of nicotine had coated his tongue. He was no longer in possession of his wallet or his keys so he supposed he must have been mugged or robbed while lying in a stupor in the street. A tramp lurched past and shouted something at Fielding. For good measure he tried to kick the dog, which cowered and snarled without conviction. 'Coin,' the tramp said, holding out a filthy hand. He smelt of something decomposing, potatoes or possibly mushrooms.

Fielding showed his empty pockets to the tramp, who seemed to find this hysterically funny. 'No boat trip for you, sonny,' the tramp laughed, and then shambled off uttering more incomprehensible oaths and curses.

A chilly dawn broke over London as Fielding staggered through its streets. How could he have fallen so low? He reached the door of his flat and felt for the spare key he kept hidden above the door frame.

His flat felt like heaven after his night alfresco. It was warm and, although not particularly clean or tidy, wasn't spotted with vomit and dog excrement. A tantalizing smell of fresh coffee wafted from the kitchen. Fielding padded through his own flat like a cat burglar. In the kitchen, dirty cups and plates encrusted with croissant flakes attested to breakfast – two plates and two cups, Fielding noticed. In the bathroom someone must have just stepped out of the shower. The room was still gloriously warm and steamy and Fielding had to resist the urge to peel off his filthy clothes and scrub off the experiences of the previous night (whatever they were). Instead he investigated the living room, where empty wine bottles and an overflowing ashtray were evidence enough of someone else's occupation during his absence. More alarmingly, the stale air bore a trace of a familiar noxious perfume and, coming from the direction of the bedroom, Fielding caught the sound of two voices, one male and one female. He crept up behind the closed door and listened to the odd noises coming from within – whoops and yelps and the occasional harsh little scream that could belong to no one but Flavia and which suggested that some kind of mating ritual was in progress.

Proceeding with caution, Fielding opened the door to the bedroom. Flavia, unattractively flushed with exertion, was lighting up a cigarette. She gave a little scream of horror when she caught sight of Fielding. Her partner lay next to her, equally post-coital. Every aspect of his figure was familiar. Fielding tried closing his eyes and breathing deeply for ten seconds but when he opened his eyes again, nothing had changed. 'You're me,' he said weakly.

'On the contrary,' the other Fielding said with a superior smile, 'you're me.'

Fielding shut the bedroom door and went into the living room. He switched on the television and watched cartoons. If he was lucky he would wake up soon and find it was all a bad dream. If he was very lucky.

VIII

THE CAT LOVER

For the Cherub Cat is a term of the Angel Tiger

CHRISTOPHER SMART, 'JUBILATE AGNO'

For Ali and Sarah

T WAS A WILD NIGHT. AN URBAN SQUALL DISLODGED slates and chimney pots while an ill-tempered tempest uprooted trees in the parks and swayed suspension bridges as if they were skipping ropes. Aeolus, the keeper of the winds, set free Boreas and he flapped his dusky wings, sending great gusts of wind across London and the Home Counties. Old ladies were swept up and whirled around in the air, like dried-up autumn leaves. The little birds were stripped from the branches and batted like shuttlecocks across Oxfordshire and Gloucestershire. Cows were blown over in the fields and pigs flew in Berkshire. All the dogs of Buckinghamshire went mad trying to catch their tails.

Boreas's bellowing lungs exhaled and his breath tore children from their cradles. When he inhaled, fishes and frogs were tugged right out of the rivers and lakes and into the skies. When the winds finally died down, the flying fishes and the flapping frogs and the newly fledged children were rained back down on the town, only now they were all jumbled up so that, instead of his own screaming infant, a distraught father would find himself clutching a wriggling trout or a fat salmon (or, in one case, a surprised porpoise), while small children were discovered everywhere – floating on lily pads, entangled in the reeds and rushes, or riding the waves as adept as dolphins.

Heidi was not concerned with the fortunes of amphibian creatures, she was simply trying to get home from work and shut her door against the wind and the freezing rain. The route that Heidi would normally have taken home had been mysteriously blocked for days now by barriers like wire cages decorated with blue and white crime tape that fluttered as merrily as Maypole ribbons. The detour took Heidi down the kind of dark lane to which evil and dread are compulsively drawn. The dark lane was a funnel of wind-crazed chip papers and plastic bags and newspapers that danced along, slapping themselves unpleasantly against Heidi's legs as she hurried to regain the sodium lights of civilization.

As if it had been waiting for Heidi, the cat slipped out from between two large refuse bins and slalomed around her ankles. A rag-and-bones tom, a bedraggled monochrome tiger, barred and striped with the colours of the night and conjured out of darkness. Heidi made the mistake of talking to him, speaking the glamorous feline tongue ('Poor old kitty') before she hurried on her way. Too late – the words had worked their magic and the charmed cat was already cantering after Heidi's heels, dodging the flying newspapers and chip papers, with the stubborn air of an animal that was prepared to follow for ever. When Heidi unlocked the front door to her block of flats, the cat slipped past her and raced up the stairs to the top floor as if he already knew where she lived.

'No,' she said firmly to the cat as he tried to weave his way into the entrance hall. He feigned nonchalance by licking a paw. He looked like a washed-up prize fighter. 'No. Go home. Shoo.' The cat gazed up at the skylight in the roof with great interest, as if a chandelier of mice was suspended there, quaking and trembling in the updraught from the stairwell. Heidi shut the door.

At three o'clock in the morning, she crawled out of bed, shivered her way along her hallway, and let the cat in.

Heidi was not even particularly fond of cats. She had never had a cat of her own as a child, never dressed up a disgruntled tom in baby clothes and wheeled it around in a pram, never curled up with a kitten and listened to its tiny snoring engine, so she was surprised when this down-on-its-luck cat made her anxious for his welfare. She worried over how thin he was, and to fatten him she mashed tinned salmon and warmed saucers of cream. She gave him an old woollen shawl to lie on and watched while he slept as if he was as novel as a new baby to a first-time mother. Occasionally, the cat would open his pale jade eyes and stare indifferently at Heidi, giving her the uncomfortable feeling that she had already been judged and found wanting by the clandestine court of some invisible cat order.

'He looks sick,' Missy said. The cat was curled up tightly on the sofa, ignoring them both. 'And even if he isn't sick,' Missy continued, 'he should still see a vet. He's very thin, he's probably got worms. And fleas. Yes, look – there's one.' The cat opened one eye and gave Missy a considered, if rather piratical, look.

'I phoned the RSPCA,' Heidi said, 'and the PDSA and the Cat Protection League and the police. Nobody seems to be missing a cat. Or rather, half the world seems to be missing a cat, just not this one. You wouldn't like him, would you?' she added hopefully. The cat flicked the tip of his tail to show he wasn't as sound asleep as he looked.

'I'm more of a dog person,' Missy said, 'and anyway, the cat chose you. You should give him a name.'

'No,' Heidi said firmly. 'Once you've named a cat there's no going back, it belongs to you.'

'Gordon.'

'Gordon? Gordon Marshall,' the veterinary nurse said tapping the name into the computer. 'We don't have a

Gordon. We've got a Trevor and a Roger, a David and a Clive, a Henry, a Harry, a Vernon, a William, a Desmond, a Bertie, a Charlie and a George. But no Gordon. Until now.'

'Does everyone give their cat a man's name?'

'Only the women,' the veterinary nurse said. 'Make of that what you will.'

Heidi and Missy contemplated the cat as he washed himself, serenely licking the puckered sugar-pink rosebud beneath his tail.

'He's huge.' Missy frowned. 'He'll eat you out of house and home.' The cat did look considerably bigger than when he had first arrived.

Heidi and Missy had done their training together at Guy's. Missy had gone on to become a midwife and then a nanny and Heidi had eventually taken a short-term contract on a male geriatric ward and, although she still thought of this job as temporary, she was now the day sister and had been there for more than five years. Working with old men, whose main characteristic was a propensity to fall out of bed or to wander around with no clothes on – usually looking for the toilet – had influenced the way Heidi looked at the male sex. She had a tendency to think of them as helpless, toothless and child-like, a tendency which had proved fatal for her relationships.

Heidi had recently finished with her boyfriend, a television scriptwriter called Fletcher she had met at an Italian evening class. They had spent most of their time together planning a trip to Venice. They had gone out with each other for nearly two years and as time went on Venice became more of an existential metaphor than a holiday. Fletcher thought that Heidi finished with him because he was untidy and lazy (which he was) and listened to alternative country songs about dead skunks in the middle of the road (which certainly didn't help), but really she left him because she hated the thought that one day he would be a little old man who would have to be tucked into bed all the time.

To tell the truth, Heidi wasn't really interested in having another relationship with a man, what she really wanted was babies. She wanted several but would have settled for one, for preference a girl and then it wouldn't grow into a toothless, dribbling old man wandering the world looking for everything it had once known and now forgotten. Heidi wished for a baby every night before she went to bed, sitting in front of her mirror and incanting the word 'baby' five times because her twin sister, Trudi, told her that was what you did if you wanted something very badly. Not that she believed Trudi. Heidi and Trudi didn't get on very well. Heidi wasn't entirely convinced, despite the undeniable evidence, that she really was Trudi's twin – or, as she preferred to think of it, that Trudi was her twin. What if, she sometimes wondered, Trudi was not actually her twin but her doppelgänger? (And in what way would that be different exactly?) Her sister had once dated a weird guy, a journalist called Fielding, who was convinced that they were interchangeable and that whenever Trudi couldn't go out with him she sent Heidi in her place.

Missy and Heidi watched the cat roll and swagger like a nightclub bouncer across the carpet.

'He's a real bloke, isn't he?' Heidi said doubtfully.

'Just don't get attached to him,' Missy warned. 'You know what you're like.'

When Missy had left Heidi frowned at the cat. 'No, I don't know. What am I like?' but the cat was too busy washing his ears to hear anything.

The cat now bore no traces of the dishevelled animal that had first accompanied Heidi home. Plump and with a sleek pelt, he spent his daylight hours on the bed, adopting a louche, leonine pose that reminded Heidi of a sultan at ease in his harem.

His appetite had grown enormous. Heidi had to leave him two full bowls of tinned meat before she left for work each morning, both of which he had bolted down by the time she got out of the front door. He also displayed a taste (shared by Fletcher before him) for sugary dairy foods and Heidi found herself in the supermarket, picking out tinned rice pudding, sweetened vanilla yoghurts and cartons of ready-made custard 'for Gordon', like a thoughtful girlfriend.

When she came home at night, he greeted her with raucous demands for more food, rooting ravenously in her bag to see if she'd brought him anything interesting while purring loudly in a brazen pretence of affection. Heidi knew it was only cupboard love but it was hard not to be beguiled by it.

Yet if he was so hungry, why didn't he eat any of the victims of his nightly pillaging? Every morning when Heidi let him into the flat, the cat dropped some small, bloody corpse at her feet with the air of one paying a rather tedious tribute. Perhaps it was some kind of tithe the cat was under an obligation to pay her. Heidi had no idea what the secret protocols of the cat order might be.

The cat was laying waste to the city, he was the barbarian inside the gate, and it was Heidi who had let him in. She had never previously suspected the variety of wildlife that lived in the city and which now turned up on her doorstep as a result of the cat's slaughtering. And so many birds! The owls and larks, the robin-redbreast and the featherweight wren, bushels of sparrows and pecks of pigeons, flocks of starlings and white doves, a secret cache of dodos, the odd phoenix or two, not to mention the unfortunate capture of the (surprisingly tiny) hawk-headed sun god Ra – an event which caused the world to go dark until Heidi helped him escape from the cat's clutches.

'Why?' Heidi asked the cat as she dropped the forever flightless body of a blackbird into the bin, but the cat was occupied with performing his morning toilette, sitting on the kitchen floor, one back leg extended like a can-can dancer, brazenly displaying his manhood in the form of a pair of tight testicles like fur-covered Maltesers.

He didn't only spend his nights hunting. Heidi was frequently woken by the noise of his dissonant caterwauling as he fought and rutted his way round the neighbourhood. In the morning he returned, reeking like a deadbeat of take-away food and diesel and rank tomcat musk.

'He's beefed up, hasn't he?' Heidi said to Missy. The cat was now the size of a baby tiger. 'But he's not fat, he's just big, he needs a lot of food to fill him. Maybe he's one of those big American breeds.'

'Maine Coon?' Missy offered.

'Yes.'

'Well, whatever he is, he's certainly very . . . butch,' Missy said. Heidi wished now she had given him a different name. 'Gordon' was more suited to men who modelled knitting patterns in old-fashioned women's magazines. She should have called him something more god-like – Narasinha, Raiju, Arensnuphis.

'Arensnuphis?'

'Egyptian. They were very keen on cats.'

'I know. You should get him castrated,' Missy said. 'There are enough feral cats out there without his progeny.' The cat gave Missy a cross-eyed look but she stared him down until he looked away and became incredibly interested in cleaning between his toes, extending his claws like a bunch of little flick knives, and tugging at the fur in between them.

She couldn't pretend any more. Lying on the floor, stretched out luxuriously in the warmth of the central heating, the cat was no longer the size of a baby tiger, he was the size of a full-grown one. Tins of cat food couldn't sate his appetite any more. If he didn't get enough food, he prowled and growled around the flat like a moody Tudor monarch. His killing was getting out of hand. Squirrels and mink, seagulls and magpies, a small, rather sickly-looking fox. Soon, Heidi supposed, he would be dragging home the carcasses of sheep and small horses. One morning he came home with the milk and the fresh bloodied corpse of a Cairn terrier in his jaws. Heidi wrapped the dog in newspaper and thrust it into a builder's skip in the street. She no longer worried about burglars.

Heidi never invited anyone round to her flat any more. There was nothing to guarantee that Gordon wouldn't kill any visitors. Luckily, Missy had gone abroad with one of her charges. Before Heidi went to work every day she sprayed her clothes and her hair with Febreze in an attempt to mask the cat's musky odour, more persistent than even billy-goat. Heidi had once had an alarming encounter with a flock of goats on Crete but she had talked about it to no one, not to Missy, not even to her sister Trudi. Heidi had begun to wonder if she might be one of those girls who attracted unfortunate animal experiences, like Io or Callisto or Atalanta.

When Gordon wasn't asleep – and he slept an unbelievable amount – he had the irritable demeanour of a circus cat, forced into half-decent behaviour against his will. He padded restlessly round and round the flat like a prisoner. The toys she had bought to amuse him at the beginning – the woollen pom-poms, catnip mice and felt goldfish dangling from poles – had long since been ripped to shreds. Nothing pleased him now.

One evening, impatient for his supper, he skulked around the kitchen watching her as she unwrapped the bloodied joint of beef she had bought in the butchers. Heidi had recently taken out a small bank loan to finance his carnivorous needs and didn't see how this could go on much longer. Growls bubbled in his throat like the promise of an earthquake. Suddenly, his patience exhausted, he gave out a full-throated, no-holds-barred, big-cat roar – a noise so extraordinary and elemental that all the occupants ran out of the block of flats and into the street, believing that the building must be about to collapse. Heidi put her hands over her ears until he had finished. 'Bad cat,' she reprimanded, and wondered how long it would be before he ate her. If only he would leave.

The local gazette ran a piece about a 'large cat' on the loose in the neighbourhood. Several people, the article claimed, reported having seen a 'grey tiger' creature skulking through the forests of the night.

Gordon had settled down a little. He no longer paced the flat like a caged tiger. His nightly forays had grown less frequent and he often spent the evening in, lounging regally in front of the television in his handsome purple coat. This coat, a kind of old-fashioned dressing gown, a morning coat, was an imperial affair – quilted velvet, purple with gold piping and braided cords and tassels and lined with silk. It was the kind of outfit that a gentleman at leisure from another era would have worn to sit in his study – opening the morning post, drinking coffee brought to him by a self-effacing servant. Or perhaps he would have donned it for an evening at home, enjoying a cigar and brandy in front of a blazing coal fire in the library while contemplating what delights his bed might bring him that night. It suited Gordon very well.

Heidi had seen the coat in the window of a theatrical costumier she passed every day on her way to work and it had said 'Gordon' to her, in the way that previously a Stüssy T-shirt might have said 'Fletcher' to her. She acquired it after she first noticed the change in Gordon. It happened one evening when she had been watching television. There was a late-night science programme on in which an astronomer was talking about weighing galaxies, an idea that perplexed Heidi so much that she glanced at Gordon for an opinion, but the cat was stoically working his way through a pint of Häagen Dazs vanilla.

And that was when she realized that he was not sprawled as usual on the floor, but was sitting next to her on the sofa. In an upright position. One leg crossed casually over the other. Just like a man. True, he was wiping the inside of the ice-cream tub with his paw, like a mindless bear, but the rest of his body language was ridiculously human.

Heidi was struck by a sudden thought – what if Gordon wasn't a cat at all, but a man under a spell? A man forced to don the disguise of a cat by some wicked enchantress? A man trapped in the body of a cat?

Heidi knew there was only one way to break that kind of enchantment so when Gordon fell into a doze, she leant over and warily kissed his downy cheek. Gordon's ear twitched and he stirred but instead of being transformed into a man he simply swiped her away with a sleepy paw. Heidi wasn't sure whether she was disappointed or not.

It was odd but once he began to lounge around like a man (rather like Fletcher, in fact), he looked embarrassingly naked. That was when she bought the purple coat.

He slept with Heidi now, not on top of the bed like a normal cat, but beneath the covers, his body rolling against hers in the dead of night, fur against skin, claws entangled in hair. His breath was meaty and warm against her cheek, his whiskers as itchy as a witch's broom. He was a dead weight, heavier than any man she had ever shared a bed with. Yet there was something comforting about falling asleep with her fingers entwined in the long fur of his belly, her breathing counterpointed by his rumbling purr, as noisy as a goods train rocking through the night. Every night now she swooned into a dreamless sleep, her arms wrapped around his solid torso as his huge chest rose and fell. When she woke in the morning she felt as if she had been on a long, long journey, but she had no idea where the journey had taken her. Gordon slept on, long after she had left the bed. The chambers of his heart remained closed to her and she still expected to be eaten by him on a daily basis.

Things had deteriorated. The flat was beginning to smell. Gordon was no longer so fussy in his habits. Heidi watched him, catnapping on the sofa, drooling in his sleep and surrounded by the kind of debris that only a cat as big as a man could produce. Bloody bones, chip papers, cans of lager, fur balls like giant tumbleweed. She crept into her bedroom and whispered to the mirror, 'Go away, go away, go away, go away, go away,' but very softly because Gordon could hear the wingbeats of birds and the scurrying of rats in the tunnels beneath the streets.

It was a wild night. A blizzard flew all the way from the North Pole and threw snowflakes the size of dinner plates around the city. Siberian winds tore down electricity pylons and telephone cables. Buildings were lost in snowdrifts.

Icicles hanging from gutters and sills fell on unsuspecting passers-by like swords. Fountains turned to glass, suspended in time. Polar bears roamed the parks and padded on the ice-packed pavements. The queen of the north country visited the city, driving through the streets on a sleigh pulled by six white wolves. Ice-crystals trembled like diamonds on her furs and when she shook out her cloak she left a storm of snowflakes in her wake.

Heidi awoke when Eos's rosy raiments covered the sky. She reached across for the feel of fur and found there was none. There was an emptiness in the house, more than just the damped-down sound that snow brings. She climbed out of bed and drew the curtains and looked out of the window. Huge paw prints were impressed in the fresh, virgin snow, the only tracks visible in the empty street. At the traffic lights, frozen on permanent amber, they appeared to go left. He had gone as suddenly and as mysteriously as he had come.

The ultrasound technician rubbed cold jelly over the bowl of Heidi's belly. 'How far on do you think you are?' she asked.

Heidi thought about the last time she had had sex with Fletcher, tedious, rather irritable sex. 'Four months?' she hazarded.

'I'm not sure.' The technician frowned at the ultrasound picture. 'It doesn't look like . . .'

'Doesn't look like what?' Heidi asked, craning her neck to see the ghostly picture of her insides.

'Maybe a multiple . . .' A student nurse came into the room, carrying a chart and, without turning round to look at her, the technician said, 'Could you fetch a doctor for me?' in a calm, controlled voice that Heidi recognized because it was the one she used herself when something was going badly wrong on her ward.

The technician was biting her lip in an effort to understand the ultrasound, but then she grew suddenly pale and made a funny noise as if she was going to be sick and fled the room. Heidi didn't even notice she was gone. She was too busy counting the tiny feet and noses and ears. And the tails. There were at least four, possibly five of them, nestling inside her, curled kittenwise around each other. Heidi didn't think she'd ever seen anything more beautiful.

IX

THE BODIES VEST

Only a sweet and vertuous soul,
Like season'd timber, never gives;
But though the whole world turn to coal,
Then chiefly lives.

GEORGE HERBERT, 'VERTUE'

INCENT'S FATHER, BILLY, DIED A WOMAN'S DEATH IN 1959. He had been washing the windows of their tiny Edinburgh eyrie and in an act of reckless bravado tried (and fatally failed) to reach the awkward top corner of the living-room bay. Billy was just twenty-four years old, a reluctant widower who had embraced his role as Vincent's lone parent with enthusiastic incompetence. Vincent's mother, Georgie, was already four years dead by the time her foolish husband plummeted onto the cracked concrete path in front of their tenement home on one of the long summer evenings of Vincent's childhood.

Vincent had a good view of his father's final moments, sitting as he was, one neighbouring storey lower, in the window of Mrs Anderson's flat, finishing off a supper of fried potatoes and Lorne sausage. Mrs Anderson was a homely barge of a woman, her grandmotherly bulk wrapped in a flowered Empire apron, who supplemented Vincent's rather meagre diet with a bottomless cornucopia of custard creams and bread and dripping. Mrs Anderson's small polished flat, scalloped everywhere with beige crochet mats and antimacassars and perfumed with Lifebuoy and fried mince, was a haven of domestic bliss compared to Vincent's own home. For all Billy's efforts at housekeeping, father and son occupied a dingy sett in which every available surface seemed to be crumbed with cigarette ash and desiccated fragments of pan loaf. Their clothes, washed to a uniform scummy grey, were hung to dry on the pulley above the gas cooker so that the scent of fried bacon was always on their skin.

Worst of all, perhaps, were the bed sheets, unwashed from one month to the next, pastel-striped flannelette on which no pastel stripes were now discernible and which were heavily impregnated with tangy male aromas. Vincent shared a bed with Billy even though there was a small box bed in the wall that would have done very well for him if it hadn't been occupied by an old dismembered BSA motorbike.

The windows, the cause of Vincent's orphan status at the tender age of six, had not been washed since his mother's funeral, when Mrs Anderson had paid her own window cleaner to take care of them as a mark of respect. Vincent was two years old when Georgie died and had no memory of her at all so that what he felt was her absence rather than her loss. Vincent had an image of what life would have been like if his mother had lived. It involved living in a warm house and eating fruit and grilled chops, wearing clean, ironed pyjamas and sitting in front of a blazing coal fire while Georgie read out loud to him from the *Dandy*. Both Billy and Mrs Anderson implied, in their own ways, that it wouldn't necessarily be like that if Georgie was still around. 'Georgie was . . . flighty,' Mrs Anderson said, searching for an enigmatic word, so that Vincent imagined his mother as a ball of feathers wafted on a kindly wind.

Scant evidence remained of Billy and Georgie's existence as a couple, only a photograph on the sideboard in a tarnished frame that showed them on their wedding-day looking far too young to make solemn vows about anything, let alone the rest of their lives. Billy was eighteen, Georgie sixteen. 'Already up the duff,' Billy explained sadly to Vincent when they occasionally contemplated this photograph together. In her cheap knee-length bridal white, bird-boned Georgie looked as though she was attending her confirmation, not her wedding, while Billy's jockey physique was ill-fitted to his borrowed suit. Even their names hinted at a childishness they would never grow out of. When Vincent himself was grown-up, he wondered if this was why they had given their unlooked-for son such a mature name – although later still Vincent suspected that he might have been named for the Vincent Rapide motorbike. As with most things to do with Billy and Georgie, it was too late to ask. Vincent supposed he was lucky he hadn't been called 'Norton'.

Many years after their absurdly untimely deaths, Vincent

came into possession of their wedding certificate, but the 'William Stanley Petrie' and 'Georgina Rose Shaw' who were incorporated at Gretna Green in 1953 seemed to have little to do with the happy-go-luckily named Billy and Georgie of that nuptial photograph with their cheery smiles and accident-prone natures.

No one ever really discovered what happened to Georgie, of course. The way Billy told it she went out one evening and never came back – a simple narrative that explained nothing. Mrs Anderson's version of the tale was more complex – his mother had gone out for a drink with some friends, she was a 'very friendly' girl apparently, and had been found in a close the next morning by a milkman, strangled with one of her own stockings. 'No one deserved that,' Mrs Anderson sometimes said to Vincent, in a way that suggested his mother might have deserved other bad things that fell only slightly short of murder by persons unknown.

The last of the fried potatoes were cold and ketchup-sodden and Vincent's appetite had already moved on to a plate of snowballs sitting pristinely on Mrs Anderson's checked cloth when his father fell past the window like a wet sand-bag. Billy's end had been presaged by the watery arc and clank of his galvanized bucket a split second before Billy himself was pushed into space by the invisible hand of fate. Billy made no sound at all except for the muffled thud of his landing, a strangely anticlimactic noise like a shell failing to explode. Mrs Anderson, in a moment of elderly distraction, muttered, 'There he goes again,' as if Billy annoyed her on a regular basis with his giddy antics. Vincent had expected to look out of the window and see Billy laughing and dusting himself off and was surprised when all he saw was a crumpled heap, not immediately recognizable as his father.

Like Georgie before him, Billy was cremated, leaving nothing for Vincent but a few atoms dancing on the air.

Someone, somehow, traced Georgie's parents, or 'Mr and Mrs Shaw' as they seemed to prefer to be called. (It was with some difficulty that Mrs Shaw finally settled on 'Grandmother' as an acceptable epithet.) Mr and Mrs Shaw ran a guest house in Scarborough called (somewhat mendaciously) 'Sea-View'. They accepted Vincent into their lives with considerable reluctance. 'You were the last thing we were expecting,' Mrs Shaw said, as if Vincent was a disappointment rather than a surprise.

A small attic room was cleared for Vincent. Georgie's old room had already been turned into a guest bedroom after Mr and Mrs Shaw decided some time ago that Georgie wasn't coming home. (They were right.) The last her parents had seen of Georgie was when she left the house one evening to go to the pictures with a girlfriend and never came back. It seemed disappearing was more of a personality trait than a consequence for Vincent's mother, although of course it later emerged that she hadn't met the girlfriend nor gone to the pictures but had run off with a fairground worker, a weasel-faced youth who had spun her round on the waltzer before leading her astray on the beach. 'A greasy Gypsy,' according to Mrs Shaw. It was some time before Vincent understood that she was talking about Billy, his father. Vincent didn't think that Billy was actually a Gypsy. He may have led an itinerant life but he had looked and spoken like a badly nourished Scot.

Mr and Mrs Shaw had never met Billy, of course, and in their version of Georgie's life he was a swarthy ogre of a man who had carried off their not very innocent child. Even her own parents had to admit that Georgie was a 'bit of a handful'. Nonetheless, Georgie had been in possession of a school certificate and good RSA speeds (junior secretary in the planning offices of Scarborough district council!), and had had a future ahead of her as the wife of some respectable East Coast burgher, instead of which she had debunked with a microscopic Vincent in her belly and fled to Gretna Green.

'She didn't have to do that,' Mrs Shaw told Vincent irritably. 'We would have stood by her. Someone would have adopted you.'

Mrs Shaw 'ran a tight ship' at the guest house and Mr Shaw, a man somewhat lacking in personality, remained firmly second-in-command to his wife, fetching and carrying breakfasts and coal scuttles and wholesale boxes of breakfast cereals. Mealtimes for guests were announced with a gong and were served with commendable precision by Mr Shaw and a squint-eyed girl called Lorna who slipped Vincent forbidden chocolate digestives when Mrs Shaw wasn't looking. Vincent and Lorna ate together in the kitchen at odd hours in between the gong, dining on toast and marmalade – a more palatable meal, they both agreed, than the leftovers Mrs Shaw expected them to eat.

Sea-View was a veritable reliquary of Georgie's effects – a scratched and muddied hockey stick in the tool shed, her first pair of Start-rite sandals in a sideboard drawer. Her autograph book ('Georgie Shaw's book – do not read on pain of death!') nestled amongst Mr Shaw's Flanders and Swann records and contained the mundane testimonials of her classmates ('Roses are red, violets are blue, sugar is sweet and so are you' being the favourite token of no fewer than four of her secondary-school *consœurs*). Vincent was particularly intrigued by the countless well-kept albums of photographs that charted Georgie's progress from premature birth but stopped slightly short of her premature death.

Many of Georgie's girlish possessions had been boxed up and placed in the cellar where sea air and mildew had wreaked havoc on them. Her jewellery case, a musical box with a pert ballerina on the top, had rusted so much that the dancer now executed her pirouettes with an odd jerky intensity to the discordant music of metal grating on metal. Vincent was sad that he would never know what tune had once played on the box. ('*Au Clair De La Lune?*' Mr Shaw hazarded with little conviction.) Georgie's books – stories of wholesome, enterprising boarding-school girls with bemusing names like Jinty and Jax and Pippa – had become foxed and limp and smelt of earth.

Her collection of expensive dolls – sitting now on an ottoman in the Shaws' bedroom – had weathered better. Pale-faced and rosebud-lipped, they wore inscrutable expressions as they waited stoically for their owner to return. Vincent was forbidden to play with the dolls as the Shaws had developed a fear that his puny body and pale adenoidal countenance put him at risk of turning into a 'fairy' – a fate that sounded infinitely more attractive to Vincent than one where he was harried and bullied at school and largely overlooked at home, especially after Lorna left abruptly one morning after being discovered by Mrs Shaw in one of the guest bedrooms doing something unspeakable with Mr Shaw. Mr Shaw was allowed to stay on but from then on was treated by Mrs Shaw as little more than a deckhand.

From his attic perch, Vincent observed the family life he had always been denied – guests coming and going with their burdens of rubber buckets and spades, fishing nets and beach balls. The fighting, pinching, squealing children, the fretful mothers, the holidaying patresfamilias attempting to sustain bonhomie – it all looked as mysterious as the adventures of Jinty. The Shaws never took Vincent to the beach, a place they held in contempt, and he was almost a teenager before it struck him that he could go there any time he wanted, although he hardly ever did as the front was too disturbing – full of noise and sweat and stickiness. Vincent did not like the sea. He did not see a limitless grey horizon, he saw a careless edge over which anyone might fall and vanish into an infinite limbo.

Vincent's little bedroom was four storeys up so that he was able to get a good idea of how far Billy himself had fallen on his final day. Sometimes Vincent viewed it from the other way round – standing on the pavement looking up and trying to imagine what the expression on his father's face must have been when he found himself plunging to earth like a suddenly flightless bird. Vincent supposed it was one of astonishment.

Vincent had formed a theory – at the moment of death, he believed, a person would be doing the very thing that would have made him happiest in life. He hadn't known Billy well enough to be sure what that might have been but decided, in the absence of proof otherwise, that Billy flew off to his end on the seat of a 1952 Royal Enfield Bullet, a smile of bliss transforming his peaky face.

The Shaws liked Vincent best when he was quiet so he spent the rest of his childhood keeping out of the way. He became a bookish boy, introverted and obsessive, yet slightly more sanguine than might have been expected. When he was eventually accepted into a more than half-decent university to read English, Mrs Shaw remarked – by way of congratulation – that he must have got his brains from his mother, because he certainly hadn't got them from his father.

Mr and Mrs Shaw died in their separate beds many years later and long after Sea-View and its contents had gone up in flames while they were away visiting Mrs Shaw's sister in Warrington. When Vincent received the news of the fire he thought sadly of Georgie's dolls, their nylon hair incandescent, their patient plastic faces melting like candle wax. He thought, too, of Jinty and Jax and Pippa, once game for anything and now reduced to papery ash. Most of all he felt for the pert ballerina, her tiny foot stilled for ever, mid-pirouette. There was not even one photograph of Georgie left now. Vincent's mother had been successfully erased from history. Vincent did not dwell on this tragedy, however, because at the time that the last earthly relics of Georgie were being carbonized he was having round-the-clock sex with Nanci Zane and fearing that his brain might actually explode with ecstasy.

Vincent met Nanci Zane on a passenger ferry bound for Crete when she came to his aid during a panic attack ('Hi, I'm Nanci with an "i" – breathe into this paper bag'). Nanci-with-an-i diagnosed agoraphobia caused by being afloat on so much sea. This was 1977 and Nanci was on a world tour after college ('Berkeley – English major'), travelling alone except for a huge rucksack that Vincent could barely lift. Nanci thought Vincent was cute. She mistook his timidity for reserve, his neuroses for eccentricity, his self-deprecating irony for sparkling wit – in short, he was the perfect English gentleman, particularly if you were an orthodontist's daughter from Sacramento who had never met an English gentleman before, perfect or otherwise.

In Crete they wandered round cities unoccupied for three thousand years and then travelled to Athens where they took refuge from the heat in endless museums, and then finally on to Italy where, arm in arm, they walked the ghostly streets of Pompeii and Herculaneum. By the time they boarded a train in Naples, Nanci declared herself thoroughly sick of the ancient world 'which was all about death' and said she never wanted to see another funerary urn or death mask or indecipherable inscription, and so they missed out Rome, which Vincent had been looking forward to, and stayed on the train all the way to Ostend, by which time they had each declared themselves in love with the other and Vincent thought that was better than Rome any day.

Vincent was bewitched by Nanci's foreignness. For starters, she had a name beginning with a 'Z' (or a 'Zee', in Nanci's American alphabet) and was almost unnaturally healthy – not only a vegetarian but a devotee of almost every form of exercise that Vincent had heard of and several he had not, the first person he'd ever met who did 'aerobics', something which at first Vincent thought had to do with airborne germs. She was also the first person Vincent had ever encountered with perfect teeth, teeth which 'Dad' had devoted much of his spare time to and which were indeed pearly – something Vincent had presumed was a figure of speech until he saw Nanci's small, opalescent molars and incisors. Her skin seemed to have been buffed and polished, and it retained its California blush even beneath the alien London skies to which he subjected her while he finished his doctoral thesis – 'Body and Soul: the transcendence of death in Metaphysical Poetry'. ('Wow,' Nanci said, 'sounds cool.') Nanci 'wrote a little poetry' too but it tended towards Hallmark rather than Plath. Vincent told her it showed fantastic promise.

Nanci 're-rowted' her world tour after Crete and went back to England with Vincent, sharing the poky flat he rented in one of the outer circles of London, her wanderlust temporarily on hold while she took a course in art history and cooked complex complementary-protein meals from the *Moosewood Cookbook* before demanding energetic sex. Sex with Nanci had a sporty rather than an erotic feel to it and after particularly vigorous sessions she would collapse (for a few seconds at any rate) and say, 'Wow, what a fantastic workout, Vince,' so that Vincent experienced pride for the first time in his life. Once, he asked her what it was she'd worked out but she didn't understand his feeble joke.

For no obvious reason that Vincent could discern, Nanci suggested they get married, which they did with absolutely no fuss in a register office. Nanci wore a dirndl skirt, a denim shirt and a crocheted waistcoat and braided her brown hair in two thick Saxon plaits. For her bouquet she carried a bunch of daffodils, and was congratulated by a horde of friends all of whom she had accumulated with consummate ease in six months of living in London. Nanci herself was the only friend of Vincent's at the wedding.

Vincent had absolutely no idea what Nanci saw in him but presuming it must be something to do with his Englishness (he was no longer recognizable as a Scot) he tried to play to his strengths – buying tweedy jackets with elbow patches, wearing spectacles he didn't really need and riding an old 1950s bicycle to and from Goldsmiths where he was now a junior lecturer.

Vincent and his new bride planned to abandon their damp English abode at the end of the academic year and take a trip to California from which Vincent hoped very much that they wouldn't return. Nanci's family couldn't wait to meet Vincent, apparently. The orthodontist had seven daughters who all, from photographic evidence, looked just like Nanci, who was the youngest. Vincent thought of them as the Zane Sisters, like septuplets or a singing troupe. Or the Pleiades. The whole family, even a couple of aunts, wrote letters to Vincent, welcoming him into their 'tribe'.

Nanci's mother signed herself 'Mom'. Vincent couldn't wait to be absorbed into their miraculous, mysterious midst. He wondered if he could change his name to theirs – 'Vince Zane' sounded so much more interesting (a cowboy or a gangster perhaps) than Vincent Petrie. His surname was the only thing that remained of his father now. 'And you,' Nanci said. 'You're his legacy, too, honey.'

Nanci had a rogue wisdom tooth which was the subject of endless professional-sounding conversations on the phone with her father in California, during which they debated whether she should wait for him to fix it or put herself in the hands of a dentist to whom she was a stranger. Nanci was the favourite child of 'Dad' and consulted him about most things, tooth-related or not. In the end, the tooth became so painful that Nanci opted to have it done by an NHS dentist. Her father recommended full anaesthesia although the NHS dentist took some persuading, accustomed as he was to inflicting pain.

Vincent was giving a tutorial when the police arrived, a male and a female constable, who hovered politely on the threshold of the room as if they couldn't bring themselves to interrupt his ramblings on Henry Vaughan. They came with supportive expressions already fixed on their faces. Vincent had a surge of guilt at the sight of them although the last illegal thing he had done was to try – and fail – to smoke a joint in 1973.

They explained everything very carefully to him in the car on the way to the hospital but try as he might Vincent couldn't understand what they were saying. Even in the mortuary where he identified Nanci's body he still couldn't understand why she lay insensible and waxy with a large hospital sheet pulled up to her chin. 'Just like a corpse,' he said to the policewoman, who frowned and stared at the floor. Vincent was expecting Nanci to fling the sheet off and jump off the hospital trolley. But she didn't because she'd had a massive reaction to the anaesthetic in the dentist's chair and her heart had stopped and could not be persuaded to start again.

Nanci's family asked Vincent if he would mind if her body was shipped back to Sacramento and, seeing as there were so many more of them than there was of him, he felt it would be churlish to refuse. The day Nanci was flown away in the cargo hold of an America-bound Boeing he spent his last minutes with her alone in the Co-operative Funeral Home. He had considered snipping off one of her plaits as a keepsake, the bright hair about the bone and so on, but in the end had decided it might look too obvious and anyway he wanted something more essential, something coralline or chalky – the bedrock of Nanci-with-an-i. To this end he came armed with bolt-cutters, purchased as furtively as a murder weapon from a local ironmonger. 'Sorry about this,' Vincent whispered to a silently decaying Nanci as he snipped off her little finger, wrapped it in a paper napkin and slipped it in his pocket.

He stood on the observation deck at Manchester airport and silently saluted his cold, slightly incomplete wife as she rose into the sky. He clutched her finger in his hand. It wasn't the whole Nanci, but it was something. He hoped that at the moment of death she had found herself in the middle of a truly great workout and that it had given her the answers to all the questions she hadn't had time to ask.

'A relative?' a woman on the observation deck asked him as he gazed like an augur at the skies.

'My wife,' Vincent affirmed.

'She'll be back soon,' the woman said, sensing the quiver in Vincent's voice.

Vincent doubted that very much but he didn't say so.

If the Zanes noticed that a bit of Nanci was missing they never said so. They kept in touch with Vincent over the years. The sisters sent him photographs of weddings and christenings and family celebrations. He garnered formal portraits of various combinations of Zanes as well as less formal snaps of younger Zanes – in Little League livery, in Halloween rig, in gowns and mortar boards. They had strange American names (Bradley, Meredith, Jeri) and all looked alike. Vincent had no idea who any of them were.

'Mom' sent him Christmas cards, although a couple of years down the line she changed into 'Ellen' as if she had realized how absurd it was to call herself mother to a man she had never met. 'Dad' never wrote because he killed himself with a shotgun right after Nanci's death.

Vincent had thought about killing himself too but he was in thrall to such a numbing inertia that he found it difficult to do anything so decisive. For months afterwards he slept with the finger beneath his pillow and tried to dream about Nanci, but she never came. At first he had allowed the finger to mummify on the mantelpiece but it had arrived at such a disagreeable state, hard and wrinkled and so unlike Nanci's living digit, that he had rendered it – stewing it for hours in an old aluminium saucepan. This was not an act undertaken lightly and Vincent retched violently several times during the course of his unholy cuisine. He was satisfied with the result he achieved, however – the clean, white bone that was freighted with a kind of magic. Of lesser things have saints been made, Vincent thought.

Vincent carried the finger bone in his pocket as other men might have carried a lucky coin or talismanic charm. Vincent hoped that if there was a Judgement Day – something he thought unlikely in the extreme – that on the world's last night Nanci's soul wouldn't come looking for her body and discover it needed her stolen finger in order to be fully resurrected.

When Vincent himself died the finger bone was found

and discarded by his wife as part of the meaningless jetsam of her husband's life.

Vincent's life carried on. He returned to his long-forgotten native city and took a job teaching in a private school. He tried to live as quietly as possible and not attract the wrath of the gods. He died too young, everyone agreed, but in the end it was a peaceful 'crossing over' (his wife's preferred term). A virulent cancer had started in his lymph nodes and quickly metastasized first into his liver and then into his bones. At the end he was wreathed in morphine but right up until the last day was still able to recognize his wife and sons – two headstrong, angry teenagers quite cowed by his illness. He wanted to tell them that everything was all right, but he couldn't speak and besides he had no logical evidence on which to base that belief.

When Vincent entered into the world of light he was in the company of Georgie, exquisitely real and vivid in a way she never had been for him before. He was holding her hand and they were watching a flock of birds flying overhead. Starlings, Vincent noted, a species of bird he hadn't previously realized he liked so much.

Georgie herself, since you ask, was spinning round on the waltzer when her soul took flight, forever sixteen and all her life ahead of her.

X

TEMPORAL ANOMALY

The hardest thing in this world is to live in it. Be brave. Live. For me.

BUFFY SUMMERS, *BUFFY THE VAMPIRE SLAYER*

ARIANNE WAS THINKING ABOUT LEMONS WHEN SHE died. More specifically, she was thinking about the lemons she had brought back from the Amalfi coast many weeks ago and which were now quietly decaying at the bottom of her fridge. It was raining, hard Scottish rain, and everyone was driving too fast, including Marianne, because no one wanted to be on the M9 in the rain, in the gloaming light.

Marianne wondered if the lemons were still good enough to cook with. Perhaps she could make a lemon meringue pie. She'd never made one but that didn't mean she couldn't. Marianne imagined how surprised her husband and son would be if she presented them with a lemon meringue pie for supper. She imagined herself walking into the dining room, bearing the pie aloft like a smiling, old-fashioned wife, like her own mother.

She had bought the lemons from a stall by the side of the road, when they were driving back to their hotel in Ravello. That was the day they had taken the boat trip to Capri. It had been very hot and all three of them had been irritable because Capri had turned out not to be what they had expected. It was full of expensive designer boutiques and rude Italians and all the cafés were busy. When Marianne saw the stall with the lemons she made Robert stop the car and he cursed her because he said it was too dangerous to stop and she said he was too cautious and he said that she was irresponsible and she said that was unfair and all the time Liam had played Donkey Kong on his GameBoy in the back of their rented Fiat Brava and said nothing.

The old woman in charge of the stall filled a plastic carrier bag with the lemons without saying a word and gave Marianne a scornful look as if she had nothing but contempt for tourists, especially the ones who wanted her lemons.

Marianne took the plastic bag on the plane home as hand-luggage, stuffing the lemons into the overhead locker on their scheduled flight out of Naples, and when she opened the locker again on the runway at Edinburgh airport she was hit by their lemony fragrance – sharp and sweet at the same time – which reminded her of the lemon soaps she used to get in her Christmas stocking. When Robert saw the plastic bag he said, 'You'll never do anything with them,' and he had been right. But now she could surprise him, and it would remind him of the sunshine, like a gift. Or, of course, it might remind him of the road between Positano and Ravello and the heat and her crankiness and the arguments which hadn't gone away but were only waiting for the right time to resurface.

The car was buffeted by wind and the weather report on Forth FM said that the road bridge was closed to high-sided vehicles. Marianne wondered if she had a recipe for lemon meringue pie. She could phone her mother and ask her to read one out to her from one of her many cookery books. She fumbled for her mobile in her handbag on the back seat of her car – Robert always yelled at her if he saw her do that – and speed-dialled her mother's number. Her mother sounded distracted when she answered, as if she'd already put Marianne out of her thoughts even though it was less than an hour since they'd kissed goodbye.

'Have you got a good recipe for lemon meringue pie?' Marianne asked but then she never caught her mother's answer because a darkness, like a great pair of black wings, covered her car and she could no longer hear her mother or the car engine or the rain or Forth FM on the radio, only the deafening sound of Hades' chariot wheels as he overtook her on the inside lane, so close that she could smell the rank sweat on the flanks of his horses and the stench of his breath like rotten mushrooms. And then Hades leant out of his chariot and punched a hole in the windscreen of her Audi and Marianne thought, 'This is really going to hurt.'

*

Marianne could see a fire engine making its way along the hard shoulder of the motorway, its blue lights sparkling in the dark. She had never noticed before that the blue lights on emergency vehicles were the colour of sapphires. Good Indian sapphires. Her father had been a jeweller and when she visited his shop he would take out the little drawers from the mahogany cabinet in which he kept his cut gems, graded and sorted by size and type, and show her the jewels, like tiny stars, resting on velvet cushions that were blacker than the night. Blacker than Hades' horses.

The traffic was tailed back on the eastbound carriageway for as far as Marianne could see – which was quite a long way, because she was suspended some twenty feet in the air. The Audi was slewed across the road, surrounded by more flashing sapphire lights. Broken glass glistened around it like carelessly scattered diamonds. An ambulance was parked with its doors open while the paramedics knelt on the road, treating the accident victim. A traffic police car and two big police Honda 1100s formed a barricade around the paramedics. The police themselves stood around, looking on, like a reluctant audience. The fluorescent yellow of their jackets, slick with rain, was brighter than a million lemons in the darkness.

A gust of wind caught Marianne and she drifted closer to the accident. She wasn't surprised to see herself down there, broken and crazed with blood, as the paramedics stuck tubes and needles into her and spoke in low professional tones to each other. Marianne supposed she was hovering (literally, it seemed) between life and death, her soul waiting to fly away while her body clung to the earth. You heard about it all the time. Near-death experiences. One of the paramedics was attaching defibrillator pads to Marianne's chest. She wondered if she would feel it when they shocked her. She wished she could tell the paramedics and the police how grateful she was for what they were doing for her, how kind they were. Especially as she looked like such a hopeless case from up here.

There was no sign, she noticed, of a tunnel or of a white light, no glimpse of the Elysian Fields. Her father didn't appear to be waiting for her on the other side, nor was Buster, the little Westie she had loved so much as a child. Marianne thought that perhaps it wouldn't be so bad leaving this life behind if she could have Buster back in the next.

On the opposite carriageway of the M9, the cars crawled past, their brake lights forming a slow-moving chain of glittering rubies. Marianne could see the pale faces staring out from the windows of the cars, their expressions sober with a momentary horror that would be forgotten by the time they reached the warmth and shelter of their houses.

The really stupid thing was that she had been nearly home herself, almost at the turn-off for the bypass, when death stopped for her. Marianne would have given anything to be at home right now, to walk through her front door just one more time and see the smile on her son's face when she came into the room. Why did people understand how precious each day was only once the doors to the grave had opened and they had looked inside? What was the point of that?

Marianne was on the M9 because she was driving back from visiting her mother in Bridge of Allan. Liam had decided at the last moment that he wanted to stay and play with his friends rather than see his grandmother. And Marianne had let him because at ten years old she didn't think he should be forced into doing things against his will. He had all his life ahead of him for that. Her heart hurt with relief that Liam hadn't been in the car, wasn't down there in the rain, his fragile body scored and raked by tarmac and grit, surrounded in his last moments on earth by strangers, however kind.

What would he do without her? She could imagine only too well how distraught he was going to be when he found out she was gone, not for a week, or a month or a year, but for ever. The thought of Liam's pain and grief produced an odd sensation, a sudden gravitational pull that made her feel nauseous, and then without warning there was a dreadful whooshing noise in her ears and she was hurtling through space, growing smaller and denser as she fell, like a heavenly body plunging to earth. Then she understood – she was being pulled back into her own body. Marianne had heard about this too, the way that the thought of those closest to you was enough to weight the balance, the tug of love that brought you back to life, back to your own life, the one you weren't ready to leave yet. She moved faster and faster, until she could no longer hear or see or feel anything but the rush. And then darkness.

This didn't seem right. Shouldn't she be in the back of the ambulance? There was no sign of the ambulance or of any of the emergency vehicles. Every last tiny diamond chip of glass had been swept up. Marianne was no longer floating in the air but sitting on the kerb, frozen to the bone, soaked with rain and being battered by the wind. Perhaps the ambulance doors had accidentally flown open and no one had noticed when she had been flung back onto the road? Stranger things happened every day but it seemed ridiculous that they should have gone to all that trouble to bring her back to life only to lose her so carelessly.

The traffic was no longer heavy and it felt much later now, although her watch still said ten past five. Marianne was sure that every single last cell in her body was bruised. A petrol tanker sped by, oblivious to her, followed by the M9 Express bus. She wondered if she should try to flag a vehicle down, or would it cause another accident? One was surely enough for a lifetime. A huge articulated lorry with 'Tesco' written on the side caused a wake of diesel-scented air that made her feel sick. Marianne wondered if it was on its way to the Tesco in Colinton where she did her shopping. She had always hated shopping, but now she would have very much liked to be wandering along the brightly lit aisles, choosing between iceberg and cos, Persil Non-Bio and Fairy.

Now that she had been brought back to life, nothing would be hateful any more, not now that she understood about the days being precious. She had heard about that too, those people who had come back from the shores of Acheron and found their attitude to life transformed so that they cherished even the wind and the rain and each and every painful, stumbling step made along the hard shoulder of the M9. The neon oasis of the Little Chef on the bypass, ablaze with lights in the dark, was as beautiful as a newly found constellation in the night sky.

Inside the Little Chef it was warm and smelt of old fat and cheap coffee and Marianne would never have believed how comforting those scents could be. Before. Before she died.

The Little Chef's other customers ignored her – a whey-faced teenage motorcyclist, two tired truckers, an argumentative couple and two young girls who didn't look old enough to drive. Out of everyone in the place, it was Marianne who looked least likely to be the person involved in a car crash.

A sullen-looking girl with bad skin was guarding the food under the heat lamps. She was eating a Mars Bar and reading a celebrity magazine that had Romney Wright pouting on the cover. According to her name badge, the girl was called Faith. Was she really called Faith or was it some kind of metaphysical statement? In Marianne's avant-garde hairdresser's, they had words sandblasted on the mirrors – 'Serenity', 'Confidence', 'Compassion' – as if they were promoting Zen Buddhism instead of ridiculously overpriced cut-and-blow-drys. Marianne wondered if Faith's badge was a sign of some kind. She wondered if now that she had been saved from death she would see signs everywhere.

'Excuse me,' Marianne said. Faith ignored her. 'Excuse me, Faith?' Faith finished her Mars Bar and yawned. Marianne leant over the metal troughs of chips and beans and fried fish and tugged at the sleeve of Faith's nylon uniform. She pulled Faith's hair, she pinched her skin, but Marianne may as well have been a breath on the air for all the notice Faith took of her. Marianne tried to accost the other customers, with much the same effect – no one could see her.

She went into the ladies' toilets to check her reflection in the mirror – to check if she had a reflection in the mirror – and was relieved to find that she had. What she saw wasn't good. Her clothes were torn and filthy, she was covered in oil and bruises, her hair was matted with blood and what she very much hoped wasn't brain matter (it was going to take more than serenity and compassion to fix that), and she had a tremendous gash across her forehead which was in urgent need of stitches. Marianne was mortified. It was no wonder no one wanted to speak to her. She picked a piece of road out of her chin and rearranged her hair to cover some of the skull fracture.

Was she dead? She didn't look dead. She didn't feel dead. She felt fucking awful but she didn't feel dead. And if she was dead then she would be a ghost but she couldn't do any of the things ghosts were supposed to be able to do – she couldn't float, she couldn't pass through doors and walls, she was cold and hungry and tired (so tired), and still seemed to be subject to all the same rules of the phenomenal world as before. If she was dead then it seemed a lot like being alive, although worse, admittedly. And surely the astral plane wasn't going to turn out to be a Little Chef?

Marianne went to look for a phone. She didn't have her handbag any more but she had a twenty-pence piece in her coat pocket. She dropped the coin in the slot and dialled home. Robert answered, 'Hello?' sounding abrupt and tired. Marianne thought he must be going mad with worry. 'It's me, Robert,' she said, surprised at how much her voice was trembling, 'it's Marianne,' and she waited for the relief and the tears but all he kept saying was 'Hello? Hello? Is someone there?' then she heard that funny little noise he made when he was annoyed and the line went dead. Marianne tried to get her coin back but she couldn't. This really wasn't good at all.

Apart from a little speeding – and how she regretted that now – Marianne had previously been a law-abiding person, certainly the most law-abiding lawyer that she knew, but given her current invisibility and her dreadful hunger, she thought she was more than justified in stealing food from under Faith's blackhead-encumbered nose, loading up a plate with chips, beans and sausages – she couldn't remember the last time she ate sausages – and washing them down with a can of Irn-Bru. She liked the Irn-Bru a lot and wondered why she'd never allowed Liam to drink it. She would in future. If there was a future.

Marianne walked the four miles home from the Little Chef. When she got in the house she crawled up the stairs on her hands and knees and went straight to Liam's room. She turned on the lamp by his bed and looked at her son. His eyelids were blue in sleep and his skin had a faint opalescent sheen of perspiration. He was in the last days of his childhood, she could smell it like a sour trace on his breath. She kissed him softly on his cheek and then she turned off the lamp, lay down on the bed and curled herself like an overcoat around her son. It turned out that love was everything, after all.

In the morning she would wake up and everything would be all right. (How many times in her life had she told herself that?) She would wake and hear Robert moving about the house. His morning routine never changed – there would be the sound of running water, the kettle banging onto the hob, Radio Scotland's 'Good Morning, Scotland' suddenly blaring in the kitchen and, just as she did every morning, Marianne would say to her son, 'Good morning, sleepyhead.' And life would go on.

*

Marianne woke up. For a moment she thought she had had a dreadful nightmare that had been forgotten on waking but then she remembered the car crash. She ached so much she could hardly move her limbs. Liam slept on peacefully beside her. The house was quiet and Marianne wondered what time it was. Then she heard footsteps on the stairs and the bedroom door opened and Robert entered the room. Marianne couldn't remember when she had been so pleased to see Robert, not for years certainly.

She strained into a sitting position. Her mouth was so dry and ashy that she could hardly speak. 'Robert,' she croaked. 'I'm all right.' Robert sat on the edge of the bed. He looked dreadful, his skin grey, his eyes bloodshot and baggy. 'I'm all right,' Marianne repeated. Robert shook Liam gently awake.

'Liam,' Robert said, his face crumpling in a way that made Marianne worry for him, 'Liam, something very bad has happened. To Mum. A very bad thing.'

Marianne thought fondly of the Little Chef on the bypass. It was the last place she had visited in the outside world. For six months now she had been housebound. Presumably, she had come back to say goodbye because that was what the newly dead did – they came back to say goodbye to their loved ones – and somehow or other she had got stuck here.

Before she was dead, Marianne would never have used the term 'loved ones', but six months of watching *Oprah* and *Trisha* and *Sally Jesse Raphael* had softened her vocabulary.

It was only television that gave her life (if you could call it that) any structure. She was glad that Robert had installed cable after she died. Now she had a narrative thread to guide her through the long, empty days. She could watch *Crossroads*, *The Bold and the Beautiful* as well as *Classic Green Acres*, which was currently running episodes from twenty years ago when Veronica Steer was still married to Jackson Todd and Gig Alexander still had hair. The characters on *Green Acres* were almost as real as Marianne's own family. In fact, she saw more of them than she did her own family. Robert and Liam never seemed to be home any more. Liam went somewhere after school, although she didn't know where because he never talked about it, and as for Robert, he was always late home and when he came in he smelt of alcohol and cigarettes and guilt.

After the initial grief and despair Marianne had been shocked at how quickly her husband and her son had returned to the rhythm of their lives. Liam still cried himself to sleep sometimes – Marianne had to go and hide in the airing cupboard with her hands over her ears because she couldn't bear it – but apart from that, they hardly ever talked about her. Sometimes Liam said, 'Mum would have liked this' or 'Mum used to do this', but then he would fall silent and stare into space and she could see him thinking how strange it was that she had disappeared so completely from his life and it seemed such a dreadful shame that she couldn't tell him that she was still there, that it was beginning to look as though she was going to be there for ever. She should have hung on to that last coin, the twenty-pence piece she'd used to phone Robert from the Little Chef – what if that had been her fare for the last ferry of all?

Marianne didn't know if she had been buried or cremated but she had known on which day her funeral took place because Robert and Liam returned home in the middle of the afternoon looking pale and numb. Robert was wearing the black tie he brought out only for funerals, and they both carried the sickly scent of lilies on their clothes. Marianne thought it would have been nice if they had brought people back to the house. She would have especially liked to see her mother. Marianne hoped they made her look pretty in her coffin. Marianne hoped that a lot of lovely things were said about her at her funeral. She wished she could have gone but there was some kind of invisible barrier, like a force field, that prevented her leaving the house.

The existence of this force field was the only evidence that there might possibly be someone in charge (but who?) in the afterlife. Although you could hardly call it an afterlife. It was more like a greyish half-life, a kind of uninspiring limbo. Wasn't it the Plain of Asphodel in the Underworld where people went tediously through the motions of their lives without pleasure or pain? She wished she'd paid more attention in Classical Studies. Or in Religious Studies, or indeed anything that might have provided some clues to being the living dead. She supposed she might be a zombie, but were zombies invisible? She was fairly sure she wasn't a vampire – apart from having no desire whatsoever to drink blood (although a good rare steak would have been welcome) – because she knew a lot about vampires now, thanks to *Buffy*. But what was she? There were more unanswered questions now than there had been when she was alive. Had she entered into a parallel existence of some kind? Or perhaps she would eventually come back, possibly as a completely different person, like Temple Bain, daughter of Digby Craddock, the shepherd on *Green Acres*.

Marianne lifted her feet so that Ella could hoover beneath them. Ella had been Marianne's cleaner, two days a week, for three years, and all Marianne's suspicions about how little work Ella did proved to be well-founded. The kettle was on before she even took her coat off and for the first hour of the day she sat with her feet up watching *Lorraine*, smoking cigarette after cigarette and drinking the cheap instant coffee that Robert bought nowadays instead of the expensive Italian roast that Marianne used to get in Valvona and Crolla.

Ella finished her cursory hoovering and sagged down onto the sofa next to Marianne and lit a cigarette. No wonder the place had always reeked of air freshener on the days Ella was in. Marianne sneaked one of Ella's cigarettes when she wasn't looking. She felt she had every reason to take up smoking and no reason not to. The bad-for-your-health argument really didn't apply any more.

Ella was wearing a pair of Marianne's trousers – black Warehouse – far too good for doing housework in. Marianne had been taking a nap in the conservatory the day they got rid of her clothes, and by the time she realized her entire wardrobe was leaving the house in black bin liners, Robert and Ella had already loaded up the boot of the car and left her with nothing but the jeans and sweater she'd been wearing. Robert must have offered Ella the pick of Marianne's wardrobe as every time she appeared now she was wearing something that had once belonged to Marianne (and still did as far as Marianne was concerned). And it wasn't just her clothes that had been disposed of, everything had gone – make-up, perfume, every last hair-clip, as if Robert couldn't wait to eliminate her from the house.

It was just as well that on the day they disposed of her worldly goods Marianne had been wearing all her jewellery (there was undoubtedly a certain freedom in being dead), including the good pieces her father had given her over the years. Now, of course, she had to keep on wearing them in case they were got rid of. It was easy to feel overdressed when you were slumped in front of *Countdown* in a garnet choker and diamond earrings, not to mention her bridal tiara, which her father had had specially commissioned out of blue topazes and freshwater pearls. She'd noticed her first grey hairs when she put the tiara on. She was sure they hadn't been there before. It seemed particularly unfair that she was both dead and getting older.

If she combed her hair forward and positioned the tiara just right she could almost hide the ugly scar on her forehead. She had stitched up all her wounds with the only thread she could find in the house (she had never been a needlewoman), which unfortunately was black, so that now she gave the impression of being hand-made.

Where was her mother? Why hadn't she been the one who had sorted out her clothes and why did she never come to the house to see Liam? What if something had happened to her as well? What if she had fallen down dead from shock when she heard about Marianne's death? She wished she could speak to her mother about all the puzzling ontological questions raised on a daily basis when you were dead. She wished she could speak to anyone about anything.

On *Star Trek: Voyager* things weren't going well (they rarely did). The shields were down, the plasma manifolds were malfunctioning and the warp drive was offline. *Voyager* was lost in space, seventy thousand light years from home. Marianne knew the feeling. She worked her way through a bag of Monster Munch and a can of Fanta. This was the best time of day because soon Liam would come home and flop down on the sofa and surf mindlessly through every channel. Sometimes Marianne managed to arrange her body so that he unwittingly put his head on her shoulder or lap and those moments almost made her feel alive.

Captain Kathryn Janeway was trying to stop *Voyager* being pulled into some kind of rift in the space–time continuum, 'a quantum singularity'. Marianne wondered if there was such a thing or if the writers had made it up. Real or not, she knew what would happen to the crew of *Voyager* if they couldn't avoid the rift – they would find themselves in a temporal anomaly. They always did. It happened to Buffy a lot as well. Once you were in a temporal anomaly everything was topsy-turvy – you would find yourself moving backwards (or forwards or sidewards) in time, or there would be a parallel universe where two of you existed, or you might even be dead and come back to life. Did the people who made television programmes know something about the physics of time that other people hadn't noticed? Marianne had a suspicion that if she studied television carefully she might find the key to her own dilemma – only last week, for example, Captain Janeway had watched her own funeral (which on a starship, of course, meant that you floated off into endless, soundless space). And poor Buffy was two months in her grave before she came back from the dead. Marianne had been dead six months now but there might still be hope for her.

She discovered half a pomegranate that Liam had left lying on the coffee table and picked at the seeds with a pin. She hadn't started decomposing – the grey hairs hardly counted. It would be easy enough for her to start again where she had left off. Indeed, recently, she had begun to feel quite cheerful again, as if the greyness of her existence was lightening, as if winter was finally turning into spring.

Voyager had escaped the temporal anomaly and Captain Janeway ordered Lieutenant Paris to set a course for home. Marianne heard the front door open and bang shut carelessly. Liam burst into the room, discarding his school bag and jacket on the floor. He flung himself on the sofa and turned to Marianne and said, 'Hi, Mum, what's for tea?' and – just like that, no reason, no explanation – she had her life back, day after day as precious and as delicate as a rope of pearls.

Marianne was on her way to see her mother. She still didn't understand where her mother had been while she was dead and her mother was reluctant to discuss it saying it was better to let sleeping dogs lie, which seemed almost wilfully enigmatic to Marianne. Marianne had been back in the land of the living for six months, six months of summer. On the telephone lines she could see swallows gathered like musical notes. The summer was over, but there would be more.

There were always more summers, even when you were no longer there to see them. That was a thought you had to hold on to.

And today they would sit in her mother's garden, which was a miracle for this dreich part of the hemisphere – a cornucopia of lettuce and beetroot and onions, of sweet peas and honeysuckle and roses, strawberries and raspberries and blackcurrants, pears and plums and apples. Marianne wondered what had happened to her Amalfi lemons in the fridge – she had never come across them during the time she was dead – but just then the sky darkened and Marianne heard the sound of horses' hooves and she looked in the rear-view mirror and thought, 'Oh no, not again.'

XI

WEDDING FAVOURS

Her children arise up and call her blessed

PROVERBS 31:28

THIS WAS IT THEN. THE MOMENT PAM HAD NEVER really anticipated had come to pass. Her son had gone. Not that far and not for ever (*I'll be back at half-term, for God's sake*) but gone nonetheless. When Alistair had left her it had been devastating and yet somehow inevitable. She was worn out with pretending that they were happy – she just wished that he hadn't left her for someone else, someone with whom he didn't have to pretend to be happy. But at least she'd still had the children. Then, when Rebecca had gone to university and moved into a flat (*I'm still in the same town, it's not as if I've gone to the moon*), it had seemed in the natural order of things and – awful as it was to think it – it had been something of a relief (*I can't wait to get away from this fucking house*). And she'd still had Simon.

Pam had never really thought of Simon as capable of independent life (*Mum, can you cut me a piece of bread?*). In fact, if she was honest, she thought of him as being mildly handicapped. Perhaps it was all those years of listening to Rebecca name-calling him (*spaz, mong, retard*). The idea of him living in halls of residence was alarming – he could barely manage to pour boiling water onto Pot Noodles. Would he be able to buy Pot Noodles for himself? (*Yeah, yeah, campus supermarket, I understand.*) He'd never even learnt how to open a tin of beans (and God knows, it wasn't for lack of trying to teach him on her part). She must buy him a cookery book, something simple, Delia's *How to Cook*. Just the first one. She wished there wasn't a vending machine almost outside the door to his room (*Oh, wow – sweet or what?*).

Pam had hoped that Simon might at least have waved her off but the thought obviously didn't occur to him and she'd driven away in a wash of tears so wet that, without thinking, she'd put the windscreen wipers on and had almost landed up in the artificial loch. For heaven's sake, wasn't there enough water in Scotland without having to create it? And now she must have taken a wrong turning because she seemed to be in the middle of a golf course. What kind of a university had a golf course? Was it to attract foreign students and their money, which was all the government was interested in, of course? She knew for a fact that there weren't enough tied books in the library and that all the money went into Sports Science, whatever that was.

She knew this from Brian (*Beardy Brian*) because she'd

bumped into him in a pub on an English department night out and when she told him that Simon was coming here he'd said, all casual, 'Oh yes, my girlfriend's son is doing Media Studies there.' And the way he'd said 'girlfriend' had made her want to punch him. Pam didn't think that was how he'd referred to her when they'd been going out together. She supposed she was too old now ever to be called a 'girlfriend' again. Ever to *be* a girlfriend.

There were *acres* of campus. If the university owned so much land why did they make the students' bedrooms so tiny? It was like making someone live in a shoebox in the middle of a field. She halted for a pair of ducks waddling across the road. She'd only just started moving again when a rabbit appeared and hopped lazily along in front of the car. Was it blind? (Did they still have myxomatosis?)

There was more wildlife than students. Simon had always despised the Scottish countryside (*Why would I want to go for a walk – what's the point?*) and now he'd chosen a university where he was going to be stuck in the middle of it – nothing but scenery as far as the eye could see. Not that he'd chosen it exactly, it had been Religious Studies here or Hospitality Management at Abertay, equally ludicrous choices for Simon whichever way you looked at it. At least with Religious Studies (Pam had been assured by the Religious Studies teacher at her school) you didn't really have to know anything about the subject. And you didn't have to be religious, in fact it helped if you weren't, apparently.

It wasn't the Religious Studies that worried her, it was the fact that he had to do another two subjects in first year. She'd explained this patiently to him several times but she still wasn't sure he had grasped it. If he could hardly scrape through his Highers, how would he deal with the academic challenges of university? If he hadn't gone to a good school, if he'd gone to the school she taught at (*bottom-feeders*), where would he be now?

Left to his own devices, Simon would never have gone to university. Left to his own devices he would probably never have left his room. Part of Pam (the bad mother part, she supposed) wished he could just stay in his room for ever and then she'd always have someone to look after and would never be on her own.

She'd never lived on her own before. She'd gone from home to university halls of residence, to a flatshare with other girls, to marriage to Alistair. Hardly time to take a breath and now look at her. She'd been the eldest of four and she'd always thought there would be family around her for ever. She'd grown up thinking her parents were immortal, which didn't look like it was going to be the case. And now she hardly ever saw her brothers (whom she didn't like anyway), and her sister, Susan, was so used to being the baby of the family (she was forty now, for God's sake) that it never crossed her mind that Pam might not be coping. But she was coping, wasn't she? She was too much of a bloody stoic not to cope. Maybe she should try falling to pieces, see if anyone noticed. Of course, they'd just give her Prozac again and tell her she was in a period of transition. Life, life was a period of transition. Birth to death. Nothing before, nothing after.

When she was at university in Aberdeen, her halls hadn't been anything like Simon's mixed-sex, shared kitchen, anything-goes place. In Pam's (girls only) halls the cleaners came in every morning and there'd been three meals a day (plus afternoon tea in 'the lounge'). She'd never appreciated it at the time – too conventional. Now she'd quite like to move back in. A ready-made life. It would be sheltered housing next. She was probably old enough for it already. Those times in halls were the last time she'd had any fun. If she'd realized the fun was going to run out so soon she'd have enjoyed it more. Was that a fox?

It started to rain for real. Horizontal Scottish rain. It was taking her all her time to negotiate her way off campus. How would Simon ever manage to find his way around? His halls of residence were so far from the lecture theatres and seminar rooms that he'd probably never bother to go. Was he supposed to walk all this way? Didn't they have minibuses? Should she buy him a bike? Would he ever use it?

She drove past a tree beneath which rested some wilted bunches of flowers. She flinched. She didn't want to think what it meant. This place had one of the highest suicide rates in Britain, a fact Simon had gleaned from the internet (*Cool*).

No, not cool, not cool at all. Would he phone her if he got depressed? Or would he just jump in the lake? (Would he keep his phone charged?) Brian had recited a litany of campus-based disasters to her – the suicides, the accidents, assaults, fires. The ghosts of dead students were everywhere. Or maybe they just transmuted into wildlife. Transmigration of the soul. Metempsychosis. Pam thought of Simon in his tiny cell-like room (did it *really* meet regulations?) surrounded by cardboard boxes, his stereo, his PlayStation, the guitar he'd never learnt to play (*Lessons? Only wankers take lessons*). He looked so vulnerable, like an oversized, ill-made child. He *was* a child, he was only seventeen, for God's sake. What idiot thought seventeen was old enough to go to university?

It took nearly two hours to drive home. On the M9 she passed one incident of road rage and two car crashes, one of which had a fatal look about it. Grim-faced traffic police standing guard like fluorescent-jacketed mutes. She wished Alistair hadn't paid for Rebecca to have driving lessons. What if Rebecca bought a car? She'd only be able to afford a wreck, with no safety features and bald tyres and failing brakes. Alistair kept his precious new family in a tank-like Volvo. They were obviously more important than his discarded offspring. Driving through Fairmilehead, past stone-built villas, their curtains drawn, their lamps lit, how warm and safe other people's houses looked. Her house probably looked like that to strangers. Was Rebecca ever going to stop being a stroppy adolescent? She was twenty and she still despised Pam (*Christ, Mum, listen to yourself*). The thought of Rebecca gave Pam a permanent heartburn. Your children were like a knot of fear that you carried around inside you all the time.

The house already felt unlived in. Pam went straight up to Simon's room and lay down on his bed and inhaled the disgusting perfume of his sheets. She burst into the kind of tears she would have been too embarrassed to cry if there'd been anyone to hear her (was that an advantage to living alone? Surely not). The cat came and sat on Simon's pillow and regarded Pam with curiosity but when she tried to hug it for comfort like a soft toy, it shrugged her off.

She woke up with a start and had no idea where she was for a few seconds. The house was cold and it could have been any time, day or night, because Simon didn't possess a clock. For the first three years of his life the rosy-fingered dawn had woken him up and he'd toddled through to their bedroom (had she really shared a double bed with Alistair? Did he ever miss her?) as chirpy as the garden birds (*Mummee!*). That sunny boy disappeared at four years old and Pam had had to shake him awake every morning since, more aggressively as each year went by (*Go away*). She put 'alarm clock' on the mental list she was making of things that Simon needed – she was going to have to phone him every morning to wake him up (*Go away*).

She made a cup of camomile tea and took it into the living room where she found a Post-it note stuck to the television screen and for a second her spirits lifted at the idea that Simon had written something for her. She put her spectacles on and read, *Remember to tape Buffy for me*. Would his lecturers be able to read his handwriting? Why hadn't he learnt to type? Would he ever actually write an essay?

She took the tea up the stairs. She opened the door to Rebecca's bedroom and glanced in, as she did every evening. Everything looked like it did before she moved out (*It's like a bloody shrine in here*). Rebecca had slept here only three times in the last two years (*I'm studying medicine – do you have any idea how much work I have to do?*). Once, Pam had had a dream where she had looked into the room and found Rebecca sitting up in bed, a child again, playing with her toys, and the dream had been so real that it woke Pam up and she found that she was crying. There was another Post-it on her own bedroom door, *Don't forget to tape Buffy* and in the bathroom one (*Buffy!*) on the mirror.

She climbed into bed, feeling bruised all over as if she'd been in an accident. She thought about the car wreck on the M9. Was someone's life over, had they been driving along, wondering what to cook for tea, whether to put on a wash when they got home, reminding themselves to buy a card for someone's birthday – and then nothing? It was a miracle that people ever did anything when it could all be over in a second. What was Simon doing? Hopefully, he was asleep and not drinking in the union bar. Or crying from loneliness and fear in his breeze-block prison. She didn't even want to think about what Rebecca was doing. Something sexual, no doubt, with Hamish, that awful, upper-class twit of a boy that she lived with. You could forget this was still a class-ridden society until you met people like Hamish. (*You're such a bloody inverted snob.*) Tomorrow she'd put together a food parcel for Simon. Would she ever sleep again?

'And as for bombonieres,' Maggie, Pam's friend, was saying eagerly, 'there's goodness knows how many ways you can make them up.'

'Bombonieres?'

'It's an Italian word, Pam, or bonbonnières, if you prefer the French. We could do them in white lace-edged nets with white flowers and pearls, square ivory lace nets with ivory flowers and pearls, purple shadow net with purple heather, Old Gold zigzag nets with gold flowers, pink shadow crystal net with red ribbon roses – the combinations are endless. And I've thought of a name for us – Heather 'n' Lace – what do you think?'

Early retirement. It was all to do with money. Sacrifice her 'valued' experience and expertise and hire a younger, cheaper teacher. Maggie, a home economics teacher, was cast aside as well. 'Look at it as an opportunity, Pam,' Maggie said enthusiastically at break in the staff room, drinking her Gold Blend from a mug that said 'World's Greatest Mum' in large, ugly capital letters. Pam thought of a picture she'd seen of Madonna wearing a T-shirt that said 'Mother' on the front and 'Fucker' on the back. How old was Madonna? Probably not much younger than they were.

'No more nose to the grindstone,' Maggie was laughing, 'no more nine to five, no more revolting *kids* – think about it, Pam – all those things we're always saying we wish we had time to do – theatre, cinema, yoga, learn Italian, join a wine-tasting class – culture!' Pam didn't remember ever wanting to join a wine-tasting class.

'And my Hannah and your Simon are starting uni,' Maggie rattled on. 'We'll have no jobs, no kids – we'll be free as birds!' A bell rang for the next period, thank God. No job, no kids – what kind of a life was that?

A pension, early or not, wasn't going to be enough to finance this free and easy lifestyle and it was Maggie who came up with the idea of setting up a business. 'Something creative, something we'll enjoy. We'll be starting all over again – new lives!' Pam didn't want a new life, she wanted the old one over again so she could do it better, so she could feed her children organic food and give them a Montessori education and do erotic things to her husband – although she couldn't quite imagine what – after listening patiently while he talked about the finer points of Scottish conveyancing law and insisting he relax and drink a large malt whisky while doing so instead of helping her prepare dinner and listen to the tribulations of teaching in a third-rate, underfunded, unappreciative school, except that in this new, revised version of her life she wasn't a teacher she was a classical violinist. With thin ankles.

And now she was going into business with Maggie, although she really couldn't remember at which point in the conversation she had agreed to this venture.

'Wedding favours,' Maggie said. 'It's a real growth industry. Little gifts for the guest to show how much they're appreciated. Shall we treat ourselves to cake? What's life without cake? Lemon or chocolate fudge?' They were in one of the many Starbucks on George Street. Given their exponential rate of growth it would only be a matter of months before Edinburgh was composed entirely of Starbucks – Pam knew they shouldn't be in there, global capitalism and everything, but really life was difficult enough without having to carry world trade on her shoulders as well as everything else and, anyway, Jenners' Café was full.

'We're the oldest people in here,' Maggie said, taking a huge bite of cake. 'Mm, this is yummy.' Pam thought she was more likely to kill Maggie than ever make a successful bomboniere.

'They're foreign, it's a symbolic gift,' Maggie explained, her mouth full of cake. 'Each bomboniere contains five sugared almonds, five because it's a prime number that can't be divided, just like the bride and groom. Each almond signifies something – happiness, health, wealth, fertility and long life.'

What nonsense. How could a sugared almond signify anything, let alone happiness? Especially happiness. People would be buying them by the sackful if that was the case.

'The nice thing, Pam, is that you can coordinate the colour of the almonds to the nets – pink, blue, lemon, etcetera. But the bombonieres are only a part of it, obviously, there's all kinds of other favours.' Maggie reached into her capacious bag and pulled out a cheap-looking brochure. 'Look, little baskets filled with foil-wrapped chocolate hearts, miniature rolling pins decorated with bells or white heather – I'm thinking artificial – dried flower cones, clown boxes, personalized mini hats, decorated fans (heather), decorated shoes (heather again) – and everything accessorized with little bows of tartan ribbon – dress Black Watch, I thought, because it's the most sophisticated.'

She felt sick. She didn't know if it was the cake or Maggie.

'Mini brass horseshoes, filled brandy glasses, filled flower pots, mini trugs filled with heather, mouse boxes filled with chocolates, then, of course, there are the centrepieces for the tables – pot-pourri rings filled with dried flowers, white lace crackers filled with chocolate hearts and decorated with little silver horseshoes, tartan ribbon and heather—'

'And we *make* all this stuff? Ourselves?' And what on earth was a mouse box when it was at home?

There's a games room and a TV room in halls, how's that? And last night we got totally trousered on diesel and white lightning and this guy Will killed a duck down by the lake so we're going to cook it tonight – how's that for a laugh, we're going to try for a squirrel tomorrow—

'Killed a duck?'

Yeah, but it was an accident—

'What kind of an accident?'

I *don't know, an accident, anyway tonight's metal night in the union so that's going to be fucking brilliant – we're going to get so mashed—*

'Shouldn't you be doing some work, Simon?'

Work? It's Freshers' Week, Mum.

Well, at least he wasn't sitting in his room on his own.

Pam struggled from the car, laden down with pastel nets (no Old Gold, there'd been 'a run on it' according to the assistant in John Lewis's dressmaking department – the mind boggled) plus ribbon roses and dried flowers and glue and ribbon and God only knows what other stuff from haberdashery (where did that word come from?). Who would have thought this was what the gods had in store for her? The mortise lock wasn't on. She turned the Yale key cautiously. Was there a burglar in the house? There was a rustling noise coming from the dining room, the sound of drawers being opened and closed. Should she fetch a hammer, or the big Maglite from under her bed – would she get upstairs without the burglars hearing her?

'Becca!'

Oh, hi.

(Why was she always so offhand?) 'You gave me a fright.'

Yeah? What's that stuff?

'Net.'

Gross.

'Are you looking for something?'

Yeah. You usually have cash in the sideboard drawer.

What on earth was she doing rooting around for money like that? Was she on hard drugs? It was easy enough for medics to get hooked on drugs.

'You could have asked.'

You weren't here.

'Would you like something to eat? Or to drink?'

I've got to go. Have you got any money?

'What do you need it for?'

I've got to get something to wear for Dad's wedding.

'Wedding?'

For God's sake, don't get all upset – he's got two kids by Jenny, it's hardly a surprise.

But it was a surprise.

Jenny's all right, you know.

'So am I.'

I have to do three subjects! Three fucking subjects – why didn't you tell me? English and Philosophy – how totally fucking crap is that? And I've got two essays due in at the end of the week. What a bag of shite. And this is continuous assessment. Do you know what that means?

'Do you?'

You've got to help me, Mum.

'Are you eating, Simon?'

Eating? Of course, I'm fucking eating.

'Calm down, Simon. You have to approach an essay logically. Get the books, make the notes, do spider diagrams, a rough draft – we've been through all this. A hundred times.'

You did tape Buffy, didn't you?

'And use the library, Simon.'

The library?

Pam wondered if she'd actually been at her own wedding. She'd had some kind of flu bug and they'd had no photographer to record the event. It all seemed such a blur now. Register office, close family, no cake, no presents to speak of and lunch in the Doric with both sets of parents. As if there'd been nothing really to celebrate. She was sure she'd worn brown. She must have been making some kind of statement, but what and to whom? Now there were girls (or their mothers probably) spending thousands and thousands of pounds on their weddings and not just the cake and reception and clothes, but the personalized glasses and wine bottle labels (*Mark and Rachel, 23rd June, 2002*), personalized everything it seemed – balloons, matchbooks, coasters, 'luxury' cake bags, wax seal kits (for the wedding invitation envelopes, for heaven's sake), silver-plated marriage certificate holders, and many other apparently vital accessories such as the 'pageboy's teddy', confetti purses, 'pew bows' and freeze-dried rose petals. And let's not forget the little good-luck charms made of twisted and plaited raffia and tied with Black Watch tartan ribbon that some poor sod had to stay up past midnight to make and it wasn't as if she hadn't spent half the evening writing an essay on 'Is there a morally significant difference between killing and letting die?' for Simon's philosophy course ('Acts and omissions, Simon, do you understand?') as well as outlining the plot of *Wuthering Heights* via Instant Messaging (*Yo, Mum*) for an English seminar he had in the morning. 'It's about passion,' she typed. (Passion! What a ridiculous idea that was.) 'An impossible love.'

Like Angel and Buffy?

'Yes.'

Had she felt passionate about Alistair once? Or Hawk? (What a stupid name.) Or Brian? Forty-eight years old and she'd had sex with only three men. It wasn't a very impressive tally. She took Renan's *Life of Jesus* up to bed with her. Simon had a book report to write on it by the end of the week. It was hard to believe that they could make them write about anything so boring. That wasn't the way to get them interested in education.

*

'Everyone has free stuff.' Maggie fretted. 'Why didn't we think of free stuff?'

'What kind of free stuff?' Pam looked around at the other stalls at the wedding fair. From here, she could see a wedding dress company ('Sposa Eleganza'), a photographer, a wedding cake company ('Cakes are Us'), 'Tiara-boom-de-ay' (headdresses), 'Head over Heels' (shoes), two hotels, another wedding favour company – 'Bits 'n' Bobs' – and something called 'Flutterbies'. 'Oh, it's lovely,' Maggie said. 'They release butterflies when you come out of church. Sort of instead of confetti.'

'Butterflies? Don't they die of the cold?'

'You're just not a romantic, are you, Pam?' Maggie laughed. Pam wondered if she could get a job supply teaching. They always wanted supply teachers. Or a little job in a café or a chemist. Or a doctor's receptionist. Maybe she could clean for other people? She was good at cleaning. She quite liked cleaning. Anything but this.

'Chocolates,' Maggie was saying, 'they all have chocolates. Can you hold the fort – I'm going to check out the opposition.'

'I doubt I'll be run off my feet.' They had been here three hours and nobody had shown much interest in their 'wares' (as Maggie insisted on calling them, as if they were eighteenth-century pedlars) beyond glancing at their table of favours, usually with puzzled expressions on their faces, and, in one case, downright amusement. Even from here she could see that 'Bits 'n' Bobs' favours looked keenly professional compared with their own. Heather 'n' Lace's bombonieres looked as if they'd been assembled by nursery-school children. She hadn't seen so many mothers and daughters together since going to see *Erin Brockovich*. A woman picked up a mini heather-filled trug and asked Pam if it was made of Play-Doh. The woman's daughter laughed and said, 'It's quaint. What is it?'

'A mini-trug,' Pam said. 'We can use a burnt-poker technique to put your names and the date of your wedding on the side of it.' And it will be crap, she added silently. She was so glad Rebecca couldn't see her doing this. 'When is your wedding?' Pam asked politely. She didn't think more than a handful of people here actually were getting married. Most of them were just here out of curiosity, yet they seemed to feel it was necessary to pretend they were on the point of tying the nuptial knot and lighting the fires of Hymen. Still, role-playing was what everyone did, wasn't it, even when there was no one else there to see them. What had she been role-playing all her life? Nice person? Kind mother? Good wife (*Alistair and Pamela, 16th October, 1978*)? Would Rebecca get married? (Please God, not to Hamish.) Would she want to look at wedding dresses and discuss cakes with her? She wished she would.

Maggie came back with a bag full of chocolates and pieces of wedding cake, balancing two plastic tumblers of sparkling wine. 'Lunch!' she laughed. A skirl of pipes announced the fashion show was about to begin and several lanky models skipped onto the Assembly Rooms' stage to music from *Moulin Rouge*. Six girls and two boys in kilts. They all looked like dancers, the kind that don't get much work outside of panto season.

After a while, all the dresses began to look the same. Well, they were all the same, really, weren't they? What was the point of buying a hugely expensive dress that you were only going to wear once in your life? Maybe that was the statement she'd been trying to make when she wore brown at her own wedding.

And right at this very moment Alistair and Jenny were exchanging vows, not a church wedding (did they do church weddings for divorced people these days? For adulterous, divorced people with illegitimate children?), but nonetheless a wedding with all the trimmings. Including her own children. Shouldn't they have more loyalty to her? What had their father ever done for them in the way of parenting? But at least it meant that Simon was in town and was going to spend the rest of the weekend with her. She was looking forward to it the way she used to look forward to high days and holidays when she was a child. How long was it since the children had both been under the same roof with her? What happened when you'd plotted the whole course of your life by your children and then they weren't there any more?

It was the difference between winter and summer, even if you didn't get on with them, even if they didn't like you, even if you weren't very sure that you liked them. When they were there, everything was in blossom, everything fruitful, and when they were gone, the world was a cold dreich place, a place like the far north country where there were no trees or flowers and the winds howled like ghosts across the frozen tundra.

'All right, Pammy?' Maggie asked, cramming a handful of chocolate hearts into her mouth. 'Are you doing anything tonight? We could get a bottle of wine, watch a video – *Captain Corelli*, *Bridget Jones*?'

'Simon's here, he's staying with me tonight.'

'You can never get rid of them, can you?'

Buffy's friends brought her back from the dead. And she had to get a job and pay bills and take care of her younger sister because their mother was dead, but unlike Buffy she wasn't coming back. If Pam died would Rebecca look after Simon? She couldn't imagine it. Would they care if she died? Would they grieve for her as much as Buffy grieved for her mother? They probably would, but in their own hopelessly dysfunctional way. They didn't want a relationship with her, they just wanted her to exist somewhere in the background (*I haven't got any clean clothes*). If she died would her soul migrate? Into an insect, a tadpole, a bean?

*

'How was the wedding then?'

OK. S'pose.

'Are you still at the reception?'

Yeah.

'Well, do you want me to call you a taxi?'

Nah, I'm going to stay at Dad's tonight.

'Oh?'

Yeah, Rebecca's staying as well.

Buffy was attracted to Spike, why couldn't she admit it? Just because he was a vampire? She'd rather Rebecca went out with a vampire than Hamish. She unpicked the ribbons on a bomboniere (lilac zigzag net, lilac ribbon and purple artificial heather) and ate the sugared almonds (white) while she watched the television. The thing was, you were always waiting for them to walk back in – not as themselves, not as they were now, no – what you expected (what you dreamt of) was that they were going to walk through the door and be three years old.

Pam wasn't sure that she liked sugared almonds but she ate them anyway. She wondered how long it would take for the happiness to start working.

XII

PLEASURELAND

Iamque opus exegi, quod nec Iovis ira nec ignis
nec poterit ferrum nec edax abolere vetustas.
cum volet, illa dies, quae nil nisi corporis huius
ius habet, incert spatium mihi finiat aevi:
parte tamen meliore mei super alta perennis
astra ferar, nomenque erit indelibile nostrum.

OVID, *METAMORPHOSES*, BOOK XV, 871–6

For Donald Barthelme, 1931–89.
Gone but living on in the woods.

WE COULD PLAY SCRABBLE,' TRUDI OFFERED.

'We played that yesterday,' Charlene said. 'And the day before yesterday, and the day before that and the day before that and the day before that and the day before that. In fact, I can't remember a day when we didn't play Scrabble.'

'Monopoly then?'

'Ditto.'

'Is that a game or an answer?'

'What I would really like is a cup of coffee,' Charlene said. 'A double espresso made with Sumatran Mandheling beans or a cafetière of Brazilian Bourbon Santos. Or perhaps a glass of Viennese coffee made from Ethiopian Longberry Harrar and chocolate from Dalloyau in Paris, with cinnamon from the Seychelles and thick yellow cream from caramel-coloured cows with big brown eyes, cows that have grazed all summer long on the sweet green grass of Alpine pastures where the only sounds that disturb the peaceful air are the buzzing of the bees and the ringing of the cow bells.'

'And the occasional yodel.'

'No. No yodelling.'

'Would you like your Viennese coffee in Vienna?'

'Yes, Viennese coffee in Vienna – that's a very good idea. In the Café Central perhaps, and accompanied by a slice of warm apfelstrudel.'

'Or the Café Landtmann? Which is where Freud took his morning coffee, not that that's a recommendation.'

'Or in the Hotel Sacher, with a slice of Sachertorte, obviously. And a string quartet playing Mozart in the background would be lovely.'

'Playing in a melancholy way? Or jauntily?'

'Poignantly.'

'How about Cluedo?'

'No.'

Taps that had once flowed with water had slowed, first to a half-hearted rusty trickle, and then stopped altogether as the reservoirs finally ran dry. Thanks to some aggressive stockpiling on the part of the bourgeoisie, it had been a long time since there had been any bottled water in the shops. It had been a long time since there had been any shops. Trudi and Charlene collected rainwater from the roof of Trudi's attic flat in the Sèvres bowl that Charlene had stolen from the museum. The rainwater wasn't good rainwater. Charlene imagined what it would look like under a microscope. It would be full of microbes and small wormy things wriggling their way across the glass slide, bumping blindly into dubious lumps of organic matter. But it was better than nothing. Anything was better than nothing. Everything was better than nothing.

'I always think vodka is a clean-tasting drink,' Trudi said. 'Lemon, ice, tonic – what more could you ask for?'

'You could ask for a Pimm's. With cucumber and mint and slices of orange and lime. A maraschino cherry or perhaps a fresh strawberry. And a little Chinese paper parasol. Or possibly a dry manzanilla sherry with a dish of roasted, salted Spanish almonds.'

'Champagne cocktails – Ambrosia, Mimosa, Morning Glory – on the deck of a large ocean-going passenger liner sailing across the Pacific in, let's say, 1910.'

'A gin sling on the veranda of Raffles in 1931,' Charlene said.

'A Tom Collins in Harry's Bar in Paris in 1922.'

'A Manhattan in the Monkey Bar in New York, a Gibson in the Double Dragon Lounge overlooking Hong Kong harbour. A Mai Tai in Honolulu, a Blue Margarita in Barcelona.'

'A Jaegermeister. A tequila followed by an Aftershock. A Brain Haemorrhage,' Trudi said.

'Is that a drink or a consequence?'

'It's peach schnapps, Bailey's and a shot of grenadine.'

'A grappa. A Gaslight or a Sazerac.'

'Lethal.'

'Absinthe,' Charlene said dreamily.

'Mmm.'

'And opium.'

'Oh, yes, lots of opium.'

Charlene had been living with Trudi for some time now. She came for an evening and never got home again. If Charlene had realized that she wasn't going to get home she would have brought some clothes with her. Now she was forced to borrow Trudi's clothes. Trudi was much shorter than Charlene and had what Charlene considered to be an eccentric dress sense. Charlene was grateful that Trudi was the only person who could see her now, especially as there was no water and no soap and Charlene couldn't remember when either of them had last washed their hair. Trudi had taken to wearing a scarf around her head, turban-style, but Charlene didn't think it was a good look for her.

They spent a soothing day recreating the layout and contents of Space NK, using only their imaginations. Another afternoon passed in reconstructing Jo Malone in Sloane Street. Boots and Superdrug took longer. The perfume floor of the Galeries Lafayette was a considerable challenge. They discovered that if they tried very hard, their olfactory memories could recall many of the great classic scents – Joy by Patou, Chanel Number 5, Guerlain's Shalimar. Others they had to conjure out of nothing.

'Number 127 created by Floris for the Russian Grand Duke Orloff,' Charlene offered.

'Eau de Cologne Impériale, created for the Empress Eugénie by Guerlain.'

'Hungary Water, created in 1370 for the Empress Elizabeth of Hungary. Rose water, first distilled by an Arab physician in the tenth century.'

'The perfumes of Roman courtesans, Egyptian mummies, Babylonian whores.'

'Mostly myrrh and animal fat, I imagine.'

There was a very bad smell in Trudi's flat. It was the kind of smell that came from dead things decaying in water cisterns or mouldering behind walls. Cholera was rife in the city but nobody talked about it much, they were too busy talking about the plague. Charlene and Trudi didn't know what people talked about in the city any more. Before the battery ran out they might spend all evening tuning Trudi's radio to try to find voices other than their own. Sometimes they would catch a fragment from somewhere far away in a language they couldn't understand. There was no music any more.

'One of my many regrets,' Trudi said, 'apart from the obvious – the dog I never owned, the child I never had, the ballroom dances I never learnt – is that I never studied a musical instrument. This is exactly the kind of situation in which it would have proved useful. I could be entertaining us now with simple songs on an acoustic guitar. Or we could be sitting together on a piano stool at a pretty cottage piano – inlaid walnut and with candelabra attached – and we could be singing German lieder or English folk songs – "My Bonny Lies Over The Ocean", for example. But sadly I never even learnt the recorder.'

'Cribbage, Rummy, Bezique? German Whist, Kings and Queens, Cassino?' Charlene offered, to console Trudi. 'Indian Poker?'

'No, thank you.'

Charlene and Trudi had been trapped in the flat ever since the night that Charlene came to visit without a change of clothes. Charlene had been getting ready to leave so she would be home before the curfew when they heard a dreadful hammering on the front door. When Trudi went to investigate she found that the door was stuck fast and wouldn't open, no matter what she did. Charlene and Trudi shouted down to passers-by in the street below and the passers-by told them that the front doors of all the flats in the building had been nailed shut with planks of wood and had large red crosses painted on them. The passers-by did not linger, for everyone knew the red cross was the sign of the plague.

Charlene and Trudi were fairly sure they didn't actually have the plague. Trudi had an old copy of *Baillière's Nurse's Dictionary* which had belonged to her sister Heidi and they checked themselves for symptoms every day. They seemed to have a lot of other diseases, but not the plague. In case they were thinking of escaping from their internment, they were deterred by the soldiers patrolling the street armed with Russian PP-93 sub-machine guns.

'Botticelli? Charades? Adverbs?' Trudi offered. 'We could play the latter elegantly or disdainfully or blissfully. Or pensively, stealthily, or even whimsically.'

'Or unwillingly.'

The cat came in the attic window one morning – a rangy, mangy, tiger-grey tom with hungry bones poking out from its dull fur. It walked across the rooftops and stepped inside. They had no food to give him but he fended for himself, bringing in dead mice and rats and ragged, famished birds. Occasionally, they speculated about robbing the cat of his prey before he had a chance to eat it, but the rodents looked diseased and neither Charlene nor Trudi knew how to pluck a pigeon and they didn't think they could ever bring themselves to eat a robin redbreast or a wren.

When winter came the cat began to spend more time indoors with them. Trudi thought they wouldn't have been so cold if the cat didn't steal the heat from their bodies in the night. But they had learnt to love the cat and love, once learnt, is difficult to unlearn.

Icicles decorated the insides of the windows and Charlene and Trudi moved in frosty clouds of their own breath. They had to wear so many layers of clothes that they could hardly move. They ripped out the useless gas fire and opened up the old fireplace and burnt everything that would burn, but they were still so cold that Trudi got frost-bite in her toes.

Charlene shared Trudi's bed now, it was too cold to sleep alone. They spooned each other for warmth, dreaming of feathered quilts and Witney wool blankets, old-fashioned eiderdowns and hot-water bottles. Trudi remembered the hot-water bottle she had when she was a child, in the shape of a small blue rubber teddy-bear. Her twin sister Heidi had a pink one. Trudi wondered how her sister was. She wished they had been closer. She wished she could see Heidi one more time and tell her that she loved her.

If they had been able to leave the flat they could have foraged in the parks of the city for leaves and seeds and berries, or in people's houses for hidden caches of baked beans and cream crackers. If they could have left the flat they might have discovered the contents of some over-looked delicatessen – peaches in Moscato wine, Madagascar green peppercorns, rose-petal champagne, panforte nero, Taleggio and green figs in syrup.

'We could eat the cat,' Trudi said.

'No we couldn't.'

'I Went to the Hospital?'

'When?'

'No, it's a game, like the Minister's Cat,' Trudi explained.

'I went to the hospital because I had appendicitis, and so on – I went to the hospital because I had botulism, I went to the hospital because I had chilblains, I went to the hospital because I had dermatitis, enteritis, fever, gallstones, hepatitis, influenza, etcetera.'

'Or we could just be quiet,' Charlene said.

'No,' Trudi said, beginning to panic, 'no, we mustn't do that.'

The gods left the city, without ceremonies or farewells. The cat died quietly in his sleep one night before Charlene and Trudi even knew he was sick. They were upset for a long time over the cat.

'From now on,' Trudi said, 'I only want good, simple things. A bushel of russet apples, a truckle of Cheddar cheese, a firkin of blood-red wine. Clean linen sheets, rinsed in lavender water and then dried in the sun and the wind on an old-fashioned rope in an orchard. A good book, a small dog, a single strand of pearls.'

'My regrets, since you ask,' Charlene said, 'include never having concentrated on rote learning. We could recite poems to each other, epics and sagas, odes and epithalamiums. We could revive the traditions of our oral culture, so long lost to us. Can you remember anything?'

'The king sits in Dunfermline town oh what can ail thee knight-at-arms they went to sea in a sieve fire and sleete and candlelight beauty is truth truth beauty full fathom five western wind when wilt thou blow but at my back I always hear—'

'That's enough.'

'Sure?'

'Yes.'

Charlene and Trudi lay in each other's arms. They no longer had enough energy to move around. Instead they gazed at the stars in the skylight above the bed. One good thing about not having electricity was that the constellations and planets were now all clearly visible in the night sky. Neither Charlene nor Trudi could think of anything else that was good about not having electricity.

'One day archaeologists will find us and wonder about our lives,' Charlene said.

Trudi didn't like the idea of being found by archaeologists. It was unsettling to think that one day, in the invisible, unreachable future, someone would dig them up and find them lying together like animals in a nest, like kittens in a cradle, and invent new lives for them. 'Tell me a story,' she said to Charlene.

'I could tell you the story of the seven sisters who became the Pleiades.'

'I think we've had that one.'

'"Marianne was thinking about lemons when she died"?'

'We've definitely had that one.'

'Her mother, Demeter, who rescued the world from

endless winter? Jeri Zane – pioneer astrophysicist? The fish that swallowed a magic ring, the death of the great god Pan, the man who woke up and found he was a cat, Aphrodite in love, the wolfkin and the princess, Tyler Zane's Broadway success, the man who turned into a flower, the girl who turned into a cow, the endless series of transformations perpetrated by the gods – people turned into bats, larks, pigs, lionesses, bears, wolves, laurel bushes, nightingales, owls, partridges, springs, fountains, rivers, echoes—'

'Echoes?'

'Echoes. Rocks, poplars, ravens, pine trees, ospreys, dolphins, mountains, white doves, comets, stars – really the list is endless,' Charlene said. 'Or how about Circe, who turned men into animals?'

'No, I don't think I've heard that one.'

So Charlene told Trudi the story of the great witch Circe, and the story lasted all night long so that on the morning of the thousand and first day they were still awake when Helios left his magnificent eastern palace, with its columns of gold and bronze and its gables of ivory, and mounted his golden chariot and rose into the sky, the fiery manes of his horses flaming in the dark. His sister, Eos, had already heralded his arrival, spreading her embroidered golden skirts across the skies.

'Nothing dies,' Charlene whispered into Trudi's ear. 'All matter is transformed into other matter.'

'Or metempsychosis,' Trudi said weakly, 'the transmigration

of the soul. Into an insect, a tadpole, a bean. A lion, a vine, a baby.'

'A star would be nice,' Charlene said. 'Or a constellation. A new constellation in the night sky where we could shine like precious diamonds. Are you still there?'

'I'm still here,' Trudi said. 'It's grown very dark, don't you think? Keep talking. Tell me another story.'

'I can't remember any more,' Charlene said.

'Don't worry, it's not the end of the world.'